FOR THE

Luxie Ryder

EROTIC ROMANCE

Siren Publishing, Inc.
www.SirenPublishing.com

A SIREN PUBLISHING BOOK
IMPRINT: Erotic Romance

FOR THE LOVE OF JAKE
Copyright © 2009 by Luxie Ryder

ISBN-10: 1-60601-507-9
ISBN-13: 978-1-60601-507-0

First Printing: June 2009

Cover design by Jinger Heaston
All cover art and logo copyright © 2009 by Siren Publishing, Inc.

Printed in the U.S.A.

PUBLISHER
Siren Publishing, Inc.
www.SirenPublishing.com

FOR THE LOVE OF JAKE

LUXIE RYDER
Copyright © 2009

Chapter 1

Hallie pulled her hat lower over her eyes, shielding them from the bright morning sun. Stepping down from her spot on the veranda, she walked towards the nervous group of guests arriving for the week. She took her time, allowing the visitors a moment to take in the stunning view in her little corner of Arizona. Ten pairs of eyes— five male, five female—eventually found her.

'Welcome to the Sleepy Hills Dude Ranch.' She smiled, turning so her greeting encompassed the whole group. As usual, she got a variety of mumbles and shy nods in response. People who came to these special singles events she ran from time to time were always self-conscious and spent the first few minutes secretly checking each other out rather than paying her much attention.

Hallie felt sorry for them. Following her instructions to the letter about the type of attire suitable for such a trip, most had dressed in what looked to be brand new boots and ill-fitting cowboy hats made of the wrong material for the time of year. Hiding a smile, she noted a lot of them wore western style shirts too. Guess they decided to go the whole hog.

One tall guy at the back in a plain t-shirt, jeans and well worn straw Stetson, seemed to be taking in her every word, as she ran through the very boring but very necessary safety information the law forced her to give them. Head and shoulders above the others, his broad frame dwarfed his companions.

'Most of this is written in more detail in the welcome packs you will find in your rooms,' she said, cutting the talk as short as she dared. The majority of the guests were city folk from farther north and already beginning to wilt in the Arizona sun. 'Maria and TJ will show you to your rooms. Please grab your stuff and follow me.' Hallie lead the way to the ranch house, stopping to allow TJ to catch up to her. 'Man, these guys are gonna be hard work this time,' he said.

'Hush, they'll hear you,' she admonished, giving the kid a smile to take the edge off her words. The twenty-year-old could be a liability when he forgot his manners, but on the whole he'd been a godsend, and she couldn't have coped without him the past year.

'Don't worry, they didn't, Miss Hallie,' he said, addressing her the way he always did. His red hair and freckles already made her feel older than her thirty-eight years without his calling her 'Miss'. 'Reckon they can't hear me on account of their new boots creaking,' he whispered, making her laugh out loud.

She gave his gangly, six-foot frame a gentle shove, sending him back towards one of the female guests struggling with enough Louis Vuitton luggage for a month long stay. 'Go help the lady.'

TJ reached the woman at the precise same time as the tall guy offered to help her. 'Let me take that, ma'am,' he said, revealing a local accent. The pretty brunette looked about ready to faint as she stared up at the handsome blond cowboy. 'You might want to change your shoes.' He looked down at her feet with a grin. Bright pink toenails peeped out from a sexy pair of silver mules with thin heels. 'You'll break your neck in those.'

'Thank you,' she gushed as he placed her luggage outside the door Maria had indicated was hers. As with all of the other rooms, it opened directly out onto the veranda.

Hallie took a quick look at the guest list in her pocket. The woman was Kelly Harding. Her application said she worked as a dancer from New York. Hallie could guess what kind of dancing from her skintight jeans and shirt, inappropriate shoes and over-made-up face, but she didn't judge her for it. No skin off her nose how somebody chose to make a living. It made her smile to see the effect the tall, blond drink of water appeared to be having on Kelly.

'No problem, ma'am,' he drawled, tipping the brim of his hat before striding away. He seemed unaware of the trail of salivating women he left in his wake.

Hallie grinned. He played the role of a rugged cowboy so well, considering the info he'd provided on the registration form, that she could almost believe he was the real thing. Aiden Jones—forty-year-old realtor from Phoenix. He didn't look like a guy who sold houses for a living. For that matter, Hallie knew for damn sure he didn't need to come to a singles ranch to find a date. Standing at least six foot four with a strong body and careless, wavy hair that just begged to be mussed, Aiden had to be beating them off with a stick.

He'd turned at the entrance to his room and noticed Hallie sizing him up. The slightest hint of a smile showed in green eyes the color of wet cedars. His dark lashes dropped as he gave her a polite nod of his wide, tanned head and turned away.

'Huh,' she said, surprised it bugged her that he'd dismissed her so quickly. Hallie wasn't accustomed to being ignored by men, especially since she'd become a widow. The local wolf pack saw her as easy pickings without a man around to protect her. It hadn't taken long to set them straight.

She'd always felt she was a little too tall and strong for most guys but they seemed to like her athletic build and unruly blonde curls. Maybe Kelly was more Aiden's type? The petite brunette had a body to envy—all curves and swells.

Hallie turned her attention to a couple of the older guests who had already struck up a conversation with each other. Rita Marshall was a widow in her seventies from Miami and apparently took great pride in her appearance if her immaculately coiffed gray hair and brightly polished boots were anything to go by. Milton Jackson, a retiree from Chicago, stood a good foot taller and a little older than Rita. His natural charm became evident as Rita gazed up at him adoringly when he stopped to help her up the steps to the veranda circling the Sonora style Lodge.

Hallie got a warm, fuzzy feeling as she watched what she hoped was the beginnings of another Sleepy Hills Ranch romance. It would do her good to remember the reason the guests—including the gorgeous Aiden—were there.

She cast her eyes up towards the hills overlooking the ranch, squinting against the bright sunlight reflected from the snow capped mountain beyond. Sharing her home with strangers would have been the farthest thing from her mind a year ago, before Jake died. The view she now enjoyed alone had been one of his favorites. They hadn't needed anyone else save the few hands they had employed to help take care of the stud ranch before his accident. Since he'd died, money had been tight, and Hallie found she could no longer afford the isolation she craved. So she'd turned the place over to the paying guests who wanted to know how it felt to be a cowboy for awhile.

Checking that Maria could handle the new residents and the questions they always had during their first few hours settling in, she headed up to her own room in the converted attic.

Easing out of her jeans, she planned on taking a shower, needing one badly after spending the early dawn cleaning out the stables. Pushing the thought of the tall, handsome Aiden out of her mind, she sighed, feeling like she'd betrayed Jake by thinking about another man.

The touch on her shoulder made her leap out of her skin before she calmed down, realizing it was only her husband.

Damn Jake! If he wasn't already dead, she'd kill him.

Chapter 2

Hallie always thought that the main problem with having a ghost for a husband is that you never knew when he would turn up!

Jake had a habit of catching her unawares. She lost count of the times she'd been about to step into the shower or jump into bed naked on a hot night, only to hear his voice and know that he was in the room somewhere, watching her. That kind of thing could make a girl nervous.

'You scared me,' she said, turning in his general direction. She'd been so lost in thought she hadn't noticed the usual clues that he was around. Hallie could often smell when he came near or feel his presence.

'What were you thinking about?' he asked.

'Oh, nothing much.'

Moving to the mirror above the fireplace in her bedroom, Hallie pulled her shiny blonde, shoulder length curls up into a loose twist, exposing her neck to her unseen lover. Jake loved her neck. His scent filled her nostrils, warning her he had moved nearer seconds before his teeth grazed the sensitive little spot just under her earlobe. She felt the body she knew better than her own slot against hers, his hard-on pressing into the flesh of her butt.

Hallie watched her reflection through lust-glazed eyes, almost seeing the indents his fingers made on her bare breasts as he caressed her nipples. She wanted to touch him so badly, but she couldn't. She could feel his caresses but could never return them. It would have been like trying to hug the breeze.

'You're so fucking beautiful, baby,' he said, lips against her ear. His voice stirred a memory of how he would look when this turned on. Hallie felt the heavy wetness between her legs increase at the image. Jake had been one hot slab of man—still was. A couple of inches over six feet tall, he'd been blessed with a shock of unruly dark hair and intense blue eyes that saw right into her soul. 'Does that feel good?' he asked, running a cupped hand down over her belly, knowing full well it did.

'Jake,' she groaned. 'Oh!'

His finger had worked its way between her legs, taking her by surprise. Not that she should have been surprised. He always did it because he knew she loved it. Hallie's knees got shaky, and she knew the urge to lie down would become overwhelming if he continued to slide his fingers over her, making her breath catch. 'Bed,' she grunted, barely capable of uttering the warning as she fell onto it.

'Did you miss me?' he asked, with a laugh in his voice from somewhere above her.

'Huh, not much chance of that. You're always here,' she teased, falling easily into the banter that had always been a part of their relationship.

'Gotta keep an eye on my gal,' he said.

She nodded, unable to say more as the anticipation of where his touch would land stilled the breath in her throat.

Hallie never believed in spirits, not before Jake. But somehow, he remained part of her life, still her husband in every way he could be. But there seemed to be only so much he could do and frustration raged through her yet again as he urged her to grab the silver, finger sized vibrator from under her pillow. His touch was enough to bring her to orgasm but he couldn't penetrate her. In fact, he didn't know how he managed to do anything to her at all, just that he could.

She often asked him why he enjoyed doing it so much. Jake said he got off from seeing the effect he had on her and especially liked to use the vibrator on her, as it was the only way he could fuck her, forcing it into her over and over again while he made her come with his mouth or his fingers. She'd ignored his pleas to buy a bigger model. 'You need more than this inside you,' he would always say. Hallie always replied that all she needed was him.

For her part, she had to be satisfied with hearing his orgasms, picturing what he could be doing to himself or hearing him describe it in breathless, urgent words. She wished she could see him as he drove her crazy with his touch. If she closed her eyes as they made love, she could fill in the blanks, seeing him in her mind.

His mouth suckled at her breast as his hands stroked over her body, dipping in and out of her groin as she writhed alone, his touch pushing the sex toy deeper into her pussy. Jake's groan of pleasure made her insides quiver, and she gave herself over to the experience. The only thing she could do for him in return was to show him how much he still turned her on, knowing it had become the way he found his own release.

An image of the tall, blond cowboy flashed into her mind without warning, tipping her over the edge before she could chase it away. Aiden's memory lingered as Hallie started to orgasm from Jake's fingers rubbing her clitoris. She grasped at her own skin as she tried to satisfy the desperate need for some tangible evidence that her husband was making love to her. She heard his breath quicken, felt his touch become erratic and knew he was coming too.

'I love you, baby,' he groaned into her mouth, giving her the sensation of tasting his words.

The room became quiet. Hallie wondered, as she often did, what the staff or guests would think if they ever heard the groans and cries coming through the walls.

'They will think you are making love,' Jake said simply when she told him. 'You are a beautiful woman. Do you think they would be surprised to find out you don't sleep alone?'

Sadness seeped into her again, brought about by the reminder that she did in fact sleep alone. She did everything alone since Jake had died. 'I guess,' she answered, unwilling to start another conversation with him about their 'arrangement'.

The times they'd talked about it in the past, Jake had said he wanted her to be happy and get on with her life but how could she when the connection between them had never been broken? He'd been coming to her for almost the whole time since he'd died. Knowing he was trapped in the confines of the bedroom they had shared made Hallie feel guilty as she thought of him alone and waiting for her any time she went away.

Her relationship with Jake was the same as any other married couple in essence. They argued and fought, laughed and cried, made love and slept like everyone else. The only one real difference was a huge one.

Her husband's spirit just hadn't moved on, and neither of them knew why. His death had been sudden, and he'd been taken in his prime. Only forty-two years old at the time of the accident, he'd been crushed by his horse, dying instantly. Hallie had never gotten over the fact she didn't get a chance to kiss him one last time.

'What are you thinking about?' he said later as Hallie pulled on her boots, ready to get back to work.

'Us,' she said.

She heard his sigh. 'I know this is hard on you. One of these days, you're gonna want to find someone to replace me.'

'Don't be silly Jake. I could never replace you.'

'I know you are lonely. I watch you sometimes when you don't know I'm here.'

She smiled in his direction. 'Hey, is anybody totally happy?' she said, knowing his guilt trip wouldn't last long. Jake had always been easy-going, preferring fun to responsibility and good times to hard work. In death, as in life, he was a pleasure seeker.

'You need a man, a real one. One that can do everything for you that I can't.' She could picture the intense look on his face as he spoke, referring to something they had discussed many times before.

'Like I said, I don't mind sharing you. It would be incredibly hot for me to watch you with someone else.'

Hallie's cheeks flamed. If she was being honest, she did miss having a flesh and blood man to hold onto when she made love and someone to support her out there, in the real world. The thought of having someone like Aiden, here in their bed, both excited and appalled her. Hallie doubted she could ever do it, no matter how hard Jake pushed.

'You are more than enough for me.'

He persisted. 'There must be some things you miss?'

'There are certain things about *you* I miss,' she said, trying to divert his attention. 'Like watching your eyes darken when you're turned on and the way your body looks when it's hot and hard for me.'

'You know,' his voice said, nearer than before, 'men don't suffer the same physical limitations here as they do in life.' Hallie felt his touch across her cheek. 'If you keep talking that way, I'm gonna have to keep you here a bit longer.'

Damn! She'd only intended to cheer him up. 'Jake, I can't. The guests—'

'Okay, okay,' he said, withdrawing his hand. 'I'll be waiting for you.'

Hallie finished dressing, knowing that she was alone again and he had gone to wherever he went. He'd be back. It wasn't as if either of them had a choice, was it?

Chapter 3

'Do we have enough food?' Hallie asked Maria as she checked on the meat being prepared for the cookout later that evening. They always had one the first night new guests arrived, giving them a chance to mingle and relax as they all got to know each other. 'There are some big guys staying this time. I bet they eat plenty,' she said, unable to stop her eyes roaming all over the back of the delectable Aiden. His white T-shirt strained where his broad shoulders met and clung to his body right the way down to his narrow waist. Buns you just couldn't help but want to bite teased through the tight denim covering his ass, giving way eventually to the thick muscles of his thighs. Hallie swallowed hard.

A nudge in her ribs brought her attention back to Maria. The woman, in her late fifties with a round, kind face and knowing dark eyes, had caught her staring. 'Guapo,' Maria said in a low husky voice, chuckling at the shocked expression on her friend's face. She shook her gray head, thick plait bouncing on her shoulder as she laughed. 'Chica, I'm married, not dead. Anyhow, I wasn't the one staring at him.' Maria gave Hallie a look.

'Stop trying to fix me up.' She smiled. Aiden wouldn't be the first guy Maria had tried to push her towards, and he wouldn't be the last. Socializing and keeping the atmosphere fun was part of her job, but Maria had always looked for signs of something more. She'd made it her mission in life to get Hallie a man.

Made no difference if she liked him or not, Hallie thought later, as she watched Kelly drape herself all over Aiden beside the bonfire. After feeding the guests and clearing up, Hallie and her crew had joined the small group as they got acquainted and relaxed a little— aided by plenty of wine and the gentle serenade of a guitar duo, hired for the night.

Hallie surveyed her guests, pairing them off in her mind. Aiden and Kelly seemed a sure thing, at least if Kelly had anything to do with it. Rita and Milton were getting on like a house on fire. That left Ike, a retired Marine from Delaware in his fifties, and Mark and Richard, twenty-something software designers from Silicon Valley. Of the three other women, Jenny was the one Hallie would have to keep an eye on. The shy thirty-year-old from New Hampshire looked like she'd spent her life taking care of an elderly relative. Hopefully Sharon, a recently divorced nurse in her late twenties and Felicity, a rather uptight, Wall Street type, would help draw Jenny out of her shell.

'More wine, Jenny?' Hallie called across to the woman determined to isolate herself from the rest of the group. She didn't look very happy to have everybody's attention on her and shook her head quickly.

Hallie tried elsewhere. 'Milton, Rita? You guys ok?'

'Wonderful, thanks,' called Rita, eyes aglow. 'What a beautiful night.'

'Sure is,' Hallie agreed, not needing a second invitation to look upwards at the view she loved. With no light pollution this far outside Tucson, the sky became an inky blue blanket studded with diamonds. She loved it best on a moonlit night, when you could see the outline of the mountain in the distance. Tearing her gaze away, she looked down to find Aiden watching her with a half smile on his face. Unable to read his eyes by the dim firelight, she couldn't figure out why he was looking at her so intently.

'You need more wine, Mr. Jones?' she asked, wondering why in hell she'd felt the need to use his last name.

'You can call me Aiden,' he said, walking over to her with his glass, crouching down in front of her so she wouldn't need to stand,

'unless this is one of those formal barbeques I keep hearing about.'
He grinned. Hallie's hand shook as she poured the wine.

'There you go Aiden,' she said, forcing a smile in his direction.
His face hovered inches from hers, and she had no trouble reading the
expression in his eyes this time as she squirmed under his gaze. He
knew he made her nervous.

'Thank you, Hallie,' he said quietly as he leaned forward to get to
his feet, so close he almost brushed her forehead with the brim of his
hat.

He made his way around the fire but didn't return to Kelly's side,
stopping instead to engage Ike in conversation. Hallie's eyes darted
around the group quickly. Every one of the women was staring at
Aiden's back, even Rita. He'd ruined the view by throwing on a plaid
shirt earlier when it started to get cold, hiding his best feature, but he
still cut an impressive figure. Aiden threw his head back and laughed
heartily at some comment from Ike, and Hallie could have sworn she
heard every female in the group sigh in response.

'Time for dancing,' she announced, jumping to her feet. Grabbing
TJ, her regular partner at such events, she began to waltz around the
fire, encouraging them all to join in. Hallie kept an eye on the guests
as they began to pair off. Rita and Milton were the first on their feet.
No surprises there. Aiden hadn't felt the need to move yet so Kelly
began to approach, making brief small talk with Felicity and Sharon
on the way, hoping she wouldn't look too obvious. Ike offered his
hand to Felicity, who hesitated for a moment before forcing a smile
and nodding her head graciously.

Sharon didn't need to be asked, taking it upon herself to walk over
to Aiden. She almost made it too before Kelly gave her a look that
would kill a buffalo at forty paces, stopping her dead in her tracks.
Sharon swerved seamlessly, grabbing Mark, one of the Silicon twins
as Hallie called them privately due to the fact they were almost
identical, and pulling him to his feet.

Aiden saw what Kelly was up to, and he took a long pull on his beer as he noticed Hallie had seen it too. 'Excuse me,' he said to Kelly as he left her side to make his way across the clearing to Jenny. 'Can I have the pleasure of this dance?'

She looked just about ready to die. Jenny began to shake her head, making a curtain of long, dark hair fall across her face in an attempt to hide but Aiden wouldn't take no for an answer, pulling her up to her feet. 'Let's show 'em how it's done. Hang on tight, darlin',' he whooped, spinning her faster as the band picked up the pace. Jenny's laughter split the night as her hair whipped around her face.

Everyone stopped to watch the show. Hallie was thrilled he'd asked Jenny to dance but he'd have to be careful she didn't fall for him. A woman who'd spent such a sheltered life shouldn't try to tackle a man like Aiden on her first time out. He'd burn her up. Hallie reminded herself again that it was none of her business.

Richard and Kelly were forced together by the fact they became the only ones left standing but the woman wasn't happy about it, and she made sure her partner knew, moving stiffly in his arms as he tried to dance with her.

'Okay, time for a Ladies Excuse Me,' Hallie called, knowing what would happen next but unable to leave poor Richard in such a predicament. 'Only rule is you gotta change partners.' She smiled, giving Rita a wink as she saw her reluctance to move out of Milton's arms.

Kelly arrived at Aiden's side before Hallie finished speaking. She was relieved to see Jenny approach Milton without any prompting, unsurprised that she'd had enough excitement for one night and had decided to play it safe. Still, it was early days. Sharon paired herself off with the other Silicon twin, Felicity got Richard and Rita took Ike.

Taking the opportunity to slip away briefly to check on Maria, Hallie found her in the kitchen, drinking her cocoa before bed.

'They seem to be having fun,' Maria said, nodding towards the window. 'Any romances yet?'

'Well, Milton and Rita are a sure thing,' Hallie confided with a smile.

'Anyone else?'

'Kelly seems keen on Aiden,' she said, turning her head so Maria wouldn't try to read her face.

'Ah, Kelly,' she spat, shocking Hallie, 'that one's trouble.'

'What are you getting so mad about? You barely know the woman.'

'Mark my words, Chica,' she said mysteriously, muttering into her cocoa. Hallie smiled, remembering again that Maria had a way of deciding if she liked someone instantly and that nothing would change her mind once it was made up.

'I must get back. The sooner I bring my part of the evening to a close, the sooner I can sleep.' Hallie laughed, patting Maria's shoulder before turning to walk away.

'Bah! You sleep too much,' Hallie heard the older woman say as she left the room. 'You don't need more sleep, Missy. What you need is a man.'

Chapter 4

'They been asking for more wine,' TJ told Hallie as she rejoined the group around the fire. How long had she been gone? Surely not long enough for Kelly to be as drunk as she seemed?

'Get a couple more bottles,' she said, eyeing the dancer shrewdly. Hallie figured out her game as she saw the tiny brunette, who didn't need to be so desperate, fall on top of Aiden.

'Oops! Sorry big guy,' she gushed, placing a hand adorned with lethal looking red talons across his thigh as she steadied herself. 'I'm a little bit tipsy.'

'Didn't look to me like you drank that much,' Aiden said with a forced smile as he helped her stand. Kelly pretended not to notice his irritation, leaning into him as soon as he'd let go of her arms.

'TJ is bringing out some more wine,' Hallie announced, 'although I'd advise against drinking too much as tomorrow is your first day in the saddle, and it can be tough with a hangover.'

'Don't worry about me, honey,' Kelly replied. 'I can ride anything any time.' She gave a bawdy laugh, nudging Aiden in the ribs to make sure he got the obvious come-on. Everybody laughed, even Aiden. Kelly was a diamond in the rough and good fun, if only she'd calm down.

'Take it down a notch,' Hallie told the band. She hoped the change in mood would help the group to relax ready for bed as they watched the fire burn out.

The first plaintive notes of The Tennessee Waltz drifted through the air, silencing the revelers. Milton and Rita began to dance to the music without hesitation, already lost in each other. Hallie's eyes misted over. How she missed having someone to hold her like that. She turned away, unable to trust herself not to cry openly in the midst of all that romance.

'Are you ok?' she heard Aiden say as his hand touched her elbow, surprising her. He stood so close, she had to tilt her head back to answer him.

'I'm good,' she said brightly. He looked like he didn't believe her but he let it go.

'Good enough to dance with me?'

'Oh I couldn't, Aiden. I have so much to do,' she lied. 'Besides, I thought your dance card was full.' Hallie gestured towards Kelly with a small inclination of her head.

'It's not nice to turn down a gentleman,' he smiled, totally ignoring her attempt at diversion. 'Please, Hallie. Dance with me?'

He took off his hat, placing it on a chair before turning back to her expectantly. The unruly blond hair he'd exposed made him look younger. Forty-year-olds shouldn't look this cute, she thought, and she didn't resist when he pulled her into his arms.

Aiden placed his hands on her hips lightly, allowing Hallie to maintain the space between them. The urge to pull away was overwhelming but it wasn't due to lack of attraction. Hallie wanted to mould herself against him, feeling every outline of his taut chest and strong arms, and she fought against the sensation. Had she become so desperate for a man's touch that she wanted to cling to the first guy to hold her since Jake?

Hallie noticed Kelly's eyes on them, and she felt a little guilty. 'You know you have a fan,' she said, determined to do all she could to bring them together. Her own silly crush shouldn't get in the way. 'Try not to let her over enthusiasm scare you off.'

'She doesn't need me,. What that lady needs is love, but she's mixing it up with sex, and I couldn't offer any more than that.'

His tone was so resolute that she wondered why he was here at all. He didn't seem to be looking for romance, and Hallie knew for sure he wouldn't need to come to a ranch in the middle of nowhere to find a lover. Watching the way he interacted with every woman he met, including her, she had no doubt he was batting above average in that department. If his looks didn't get 'em all, his charm picked up the rest.

The song seemed to last forever, giving her time to relax enough to actually feel the man she touched. Her hand seemed tiny where it rested on his massive shoulder, fingers splayed across his tight muscles. Her other hand rested lightly in his, the thick fingers almost engulfing hers. His thumb brushed over her skin in time with the music, soothing the tension from her.

She could feel his breath on her cheek as he leaned his head forward to rest it against hers. The height difference meant her eyes were level with his neck, and she focused hard on the tan skin inches from her nose as she felt his fingers bite a little harder into her hips.

'Hallie?' he said.

She waited for him to finish whatever he had planned to say but he fell silent for so long that she was forced to look up at him. Hallie didn't know him well enough to match an emotion to the expression in his dark green eyes but she felt it none the less. Her insides coiled as she stared at him, unable to look away despite her discomfort.

'What makes you so sad?' he asked. She tried to drop her head, but his finger under her chin stopped her. 'I can see it in your pretty brown eyes. You do a good job of hiding it but, every now and then, you get the look of a tortured soul.'

Hallie pulled away abruptly. 'I'm fine,' she said, brushing his eyes and his comment away. What was he trying to do? Ensure every woman present had fallen in love with him before he was through? She didn't like to be toyed with. 'You're seeing something that isn't there.'

Aiden smiled. 'If the lady says she's fine, then she's fine.' He raised his hands in mock surrender, backing away with a smile. 'Thanks for the dance, Hallie.'

She watched as he picked up his hat, biding the group a general good night before walking into the darkness towards his room. Annoyed as she was, Hallie couldn't drag her eyes away until he strolled out of sight.

Chapter 5

TJ yelled, his youthful voice barely carrying across the vast plain. 'Kelly, don't wander too far from the group,' His eyes searched for Hallie's through the throng of other riders, frustration evident. 'She won't listen to me,' he mouthed, throwing his hands in the air.

The kid was a worrier. Sure, Kelly had been a little annoying but Hallie kept an eye on her, as had everyone. Kelly liked to be the center of attention and had an endless supply of tricks up her sleeve to ensure it stayed that way. By the half-way point of their dawn ride, the group had already suffered through the drama of Kelly not liking her horse, losing her hat and screaming in terror when a bug landed on her arm. For some strange reason, Hallie found she liked her, despite the fact she was a royal pain in the ass.

The reason for Kelly's exhibitionism sidled alongside, drawing Hallie's attention. 'You want me to go get her? Hallie?' he repeated when he got no reply.

She didn't answer because she couldn't speak. The memory of his taut thighs rippling as he'd first straddled his horse a couple of hours earlier had taunted her all morning. Hallie didn't know where to put her eyes. Keeping them where they were at that moment—fixated on his groin as it caressed the leather of his saddle—wasn't an option. Her hat spared her blushes and she took a deep breath before meeting his gaze. 'Uh, no, it's okay. TJ will get her.'

'I don't mind helping out. You guys have your hands full watching all the rookies.' He smiled, jerking his head towards the inexperienced riders following them. 'You sure you don't want me to chase her?'

Hallie laughed, ignoring the challenge in his words and the twinkle in his eye. 'She's coming back now anyway,' she said, noticing how Kelly suddenly had a keen interest in their conversation. 'Take my word for it. You won't need to chase Kelly very far. She's begging to get caught.'

Thrilled she'd made him laugh out loud with her sassy comment, Hallie gave her horse a gentle kick, riding away before she had time to analyze why his reaction mattered so much.

'Round 'em up, TJ,' she called, 'time for lunch.'

Twenty minutes later, the horses were tethered at the trough, cooling down while their riders sprawled under the shade of a cluster of Palo Verdes to enjoy the picnic. Each had been responsible for a saddle bag Maria had issued back at the ranch which, when the contents were combined, offered up a huge feast. Hallie liked this part of the day. People became friends during mutual experiences such as eating together.

The Silicon twins chatted with Sharon and tried to include Jenny in the conversation. Hallie smiled as she saw Mark, the slightly heavier and shorter of the two, place a hand on Jenny's arm, bringing her attention to a family of cactus wrens, sitting quietly in a nearby tree. 'That's Arizona's state bird,' he told her proudly, surprising Hallie with his knowledge. Jenny followed his gaze, turning back to him with a shy, hopeful look in her eyes. Mark's bravery escaped him for a moment as he struggled for more to say before giving up and staring back at her with a silly smile. Hallie could almost see Jenny's toes curling in delight.

Rita and Milton were sitting alone, under their own tree. Their rapidly deepening friendship threatened to isolate them from the group, and Hallie reminded herself to keep them involved. Yes, finding romance was one of the aims of the trip, but so was having a damn good time. There was an almost endless list of activities on offer— the wildlife, riding, dancing, fishing. Hallie hoped they wouldn't miss out.

Ike was a darling. Brutally blunt, but with a heart as big as Texas, he blustered and shouted his way through most things and laughed without reservation at anything that tickled him. Larger than life in more ways than one, his big frame dominated any situation. Yet, people seemed to gravitate towards him, attracted by his strength of character.

'Oh God, he's so loud,' Felicity complained quietly to Hallie, pressing a hand to her temple in mock pain when Ike announced proudly that his ass had gone numb. His raucous laughter was infectious, and Hallie saw Felicity's lips twitch in response, despite her complaints.

'Not as lean, not as mean, but still a Marine,' he bellowed, making Felicity wince again, her burgundy bob swinging around her face as she shook her head.

'Do Marines ever shut up?' she snapped waspishly. Ike's initial shock at her outburst lasted only a second before he slapped her heartily on the back and laughed good-naturedly, assuming she was only joshing with him. The shock on Felicity's face was such a picture. Hallie had to stuff some food in her own mouth to stop herself from giggling. Felicity's throaty laughter surprised all of them. Maybe she wasn't as uptight as she'd first seemed?

After checking on everyone else, Hallie had no choice but to look at Aiden. All that remained visible of the very distracting man was the top of his hat. Kelly did such a good job of isolating him and monopolizing his attention, that she'd formed a physical barrier between him and the group as she kneeled over him possessively. Hallie could only guess at the view he had with his nose near buried in Kelly's cleavage, and she felt a little sorry for him. Aiden didn't strike her as the kind of guy who liked to be manipulated. Still, he didn't seem to be doing much to dissuade her.

The sudden sound of scolding, angry cactus wrens split the air, bringing Hallie to her feet as casually as she dared. The birds often warned of rattlesnakes, seeing them long before any human could.

Scanning the group quickly to check none of the others had caught her reactions, she found Aiden on his feet too, eyes searching the ground for signs of the invader. So he knew what the sound of the birds could mean? There was no way this guy sold houses for a living.

TJ returned after scouting the area, shrugging his shoulders to show there were no signs of anything untoward. The horses didn't seem concerned, so whatever the danger had been, it must have passed. Hallie checked her watch, deciding it was so near the time they usually turned back for home that she may as well get them all moving.

Chapter 6

The path home took them through a pretty valley surrounded by cottonwoods. A small creek bubbled through the middle, attracting many and varied wildlife to its edge. The experience was a magical one, and Hallie loved showing it to visitors. Sharing what had been one of her and Jake's favorite places with them lessened the pain of being there. She looked forward to the day when she could enjoy it again without the suffocating memories.

He hadn't visited her last night and Hallie wondered why. It wasn't the first time he'd gone AWOL. Just after his death, they had both been elated to discover that, somehow, he'd been able to come back. The euphoria hadn't lasted long when Jake had realized he'd become stuck between two worlds. He'd disappeared for a few days, searching for answers but returning after finding none.

Hallie hated that he wouldn't describe what it was like for him, what he saw or where he went. He would just laugh and tell her it wasn't her time to know yet. 'I don't want to rob you of the wonder Hallic,' he would say, his voice bright at the prospect.

A sudden shout jolted her out of the daydream. Kelly flew passed, clutching onto her horse in terror. She'd been a ways behind the group, and Hallie had lost sight of her until now. Something had spooked the usually placid Appaloosa.

'Whoa, Cookie,' Kelly screamed, as horse and rider disappeared around the bend of the creek and out of sight. Hallie spurred her own horse into action, preparing to give chase, almost slamming into the side of Aiden's steed as he careened passed, body low in the saddle, hat in hand.

By the time Hallie caught up with them, Aiden had Kelly's horse under control. Jumping down, she left her trusty mare to take a much needed drink, running through the water, over to Kelly standing shakily at the edge of the creek. 'What in hell happened?' she said, almost out of breath as adrenaline and the weight of her wet jeans combined to drain her of air.

'I...I don't know,' Kelly stuttered, eyes wide, tears making her voice quiver. 'I saw something in the trees beside me, and I yelped. I guess the horse saw it too and took off.'

'Or maybe the fact you have been screaming all day finally spooked her,' said Aiden, surprising the women at the anger in his tone. 'This horse is injured.' He turned away, unable to meet Kelly's eyes as she apologized quietly, shame making her cheeks burn.

Aiden ran his hands down Cookie's leg, speaking to her gently as she pulled away when he touched the sore spot at her fetlock. 'I think she bruised a tendon.' A nerve ticked in his jaw, and Hallie could see he was furious but holding it in for the benefit of the still nervous horse. Getting to his feet, Aiden lead the mare back into the water, knowing the coolness of the creek would soothe the joint and take down some of the swelling.

TJ caught up, telling Hallie that he'd made the others wait for his return. 'Take them on back to the ranch. It's not far now. Kelly can take my horse, and I will walk Cookie back once the swelling has gone down a little.'

'You sure, Miss Hallie? It's almost three miles.'

'Don't worry, I will stay with her,' Aiden said. 'We can share my horse.'

About to disagree, Hallie decided against it. His idea made sense. If Cookie suddenly went lame, he could go for help. How foolish would it be to refuse his help just because he made her nervous?

Busying herself with calming Kelly down before sending her and the group off home, she avoided the thought of spending time alone with the mysterious Aiden. She had no reason to suspect he was anything other than what he claimed to be, but she did wonder at his knowledge of the region and its animals, including the horses. Maybe he grew up on a farm.

'How is she?' Hallie asked, approaching Aiden and the two horses tethered by the bank. 'She looks a little happier.'

'Good girl,' he cooed into the ear of the still skittish Cookie before turning to Hallie. 'She's better but not much. We need to get this leg looked at.' He stopped talking abruptly, letting his eyes wander over her body, swallowing hard.

Hallie looked down. The dash through the water to Kelly's side had soaked her to the skin, making her white t-shirt almost transparent. Her nipples contracted as she felt his eyes on her breasts, poking through the thin cotton proudly. Her glance flashed up to his, hoping he hadn't noticed. Considering the fact his gaze was fixed on them and he looked like he wanted to lunge at her, she'd have to guess he had.

The urge to fold her arms became almost irresistible but she stopped herself, unwilling to let him know she was aware of his bold appraisal of her body. As casually as she could, Hallie walked to the other side of the horse, shielding herself from his eyes. 'Is she okay to walk yet?' she asked, refusing to look at him.

'Just a few more minutes and we can give it a try.' Aiden's voice sounded raw, and Hallie couldn't resist the urge to look at him over Cookie's back. His eyes were wide, and she could almost feel the tension in him. Was he still thinking of the way her body had reacted to his gaze?

Aiden mounted his horse, another Appaloosa called Dylan, settling into his saddle before reaching down to help Hallie climb up behind him. Although she knew better, she sat as far back as she dared, trying not to press her breasts against his firm back.

'Unless you want this horse to throw us both, you better get a little closer. Here, put your arms around me,' he said, reaching behind him to grab her ass, physically dragging her forward. Hallie's pelvis made hard contact with his butt as her breasts squashed into his back. She gasped, heat coiling through her as her body molded itself to his shape.

'Damn,' she heard him mutter quietly as he adjusted his position in the saddle. His hand moved to the crotch of his jeans, pulling at the material with a quick motion, as if trying to make himself more comfortable.

Aiden pulled his hat further down over his face and spurred Dylan forward, looping Cookie's reins around the horn of his saddle. The path home took them away from the creek, leading down into the valley through a gentle incline. Hallie almost groaned as her body was forced even closer to his when her weight shifted forward. The sway of the horse made her groin grind against the saddle as the inside of her thighs grazed across Aiden's butt, and she began to get hot. Her nipples refused to calm down, teased into life again by constant brushing against the taut, hard wall of muscle in front of her.

Hallie kept her grip loose on his waist. She would have preferred not to have touched him at all but she didn't dare bring attention to herself by moving away again. The motion of the horse made Aiden's body sway and twist under her palms, causing the fabric of his t-shirt to brush softly over his skin as the smooth muscles rippled beneath. Her insides coiled tighter by the second, and she felt her pussy begin to contract as the overtly sexual combination of Aiden and the movement of the animal beneath them began to fray what was left of her composure. Her breath came in short, restrained gasps, and she fought not to show how aroused she had become as his scent filled her nostrils.

The ground beneath them got more uneven as they reached the bottom of the hill. The horse lost his footing for a second, jolting them hard as he stumbled on a rock. Hallie groaned aloud as a ripple went through her, clitoris reacting violently to the temporary increase in friction.

Dylan stopped abruptly at Aiden's command. Before Hallie could ask why, her arm and thigh were gripped firmly and she was being pulled across Aiden's body and forced to sit in his lap. 'What…what are you doing?' she asked as she found her mouth inches from his.

'Hallie, don't tell me you aren't turned on. I know damn well I am,' he muttered, eyes gesturing towards the huge erection threatening to burst through his jeans. 'Your nipples have been digging into my back and driving me crazy for the last ten minutes.' His hands snaked up her spine, urging her body against his as he focused on her lips but didn't kiss her. She shook her head in denial. 'I didn't take you for a liar.'

She tried to pull away but his grip simply tightened, forcing her to confront what was happening between them. His almost closed eyes were fixed on her mouth as his breath came in short, hot pants, fanning her face and neck.

'Can I kiss you?'

'No,' she said, watching his lips, her body moving towards him despite her words.

'Do you know what you're doing to me?' he said, moments before her mouth met his.

'Hmmm,' Hallie groaned as he turned the first tentative touch of her lips into a full blooded exploration of her mouth and tongue. His large hand molded the back of her neck, leaving no room for escape, or breath, as he kissed her.

Her hands went to his head, knocking his hat to the ground unnoticed as she buried her fingers in the unruly mane of blond hair lightened by the sun. Hallie felt his withdrawal moments before he used her shoulders to put a little distance between them. 'We've got company,' he said, gesturing to a trail of dust crossing the floor of the valley towards them. Hallie followed his gaze before scrambling from his lap, sliding to the ground.

'Shit,' she cursed, straightening clothing that didn't need it rather than look his way. She kicked at his hat in anger before picking it up and throwing it at him.

'What are you so mad about? The fact that we got stopped or that we started at all?'

'It's not that simple. This shouldn't have happened.'

Aiden smiled. 'I didn't plan this either but you can't deny there is something going on here.'

'Well, it starts and ends now,' she said.

'Why does it have to end before it's begun? I know your situation—widowed and running this place alone.' He laughed. 'Hell, we both know it's going to happen.'

'How come you know so much about me?' Hallie asked, ignoring his arrogance. Considering the fact she'd been straddling his hard dick only moments before, frustrated by the rigid denim between them, she couldn't protest too much.

'Maria,' he said, one word telling Hallie all she needed to know.

'Maria should mind her own business. Besides, you seemed to be hitting it off with Kelly,' she said, forcing a laugh into her voice. 'Or did you plan to have us both?'

'You didn't strike me as the jealous type,' he drawled, intentionally misunderstanding.

'Fuck you, Aiden,' she said, tension beginning to fray her nerves.

'Oh, you will,' he warned quietly.

The vehicle arrived before she could bring him down a peg or two, cutting short the conversation. TJ had comeback for them, horse trailer in tow. 'Good thinking,' Hallie said, as he leapt from the pickup and ran over to her. 'It's best if she doesn't walk too far.'

She made the most of the distraction, shutting Aiden out as she focused on the task at hand. TJ almost blew her chance at escape by volunteering to ride Dylan back to the ranch. 'Bet you could do with a cold beer,' he said to Aiden with a smile.

'That's ok, kid,' he replied, eyes burning into Hallie. 'I could do with some time alone. Gotta clear my head.'

Loading the injured but well trained horse didn't take long. Hallie jumped into the driving seat without speaking to him again before heading back across the valley, leaving her no time to confront the look she knew she would find in his eyes.

Chapter 7

Hallie had been relieved she had the night off. The events of the afternoon had begun to take their toll. Returning to the ranch, she'd been sorely tempted to give Maria a piece of her mind before she realized she was only mad at herself. Aiden wasn't the first guy Maria had nudged in her direction but he'd been the first one Hallie had allowed to get so close.

She hid in her room as soon as she got home, unwilling to face Aiden when he returned. The guests were free for the evening anyway, as there wasn't much point planning events for people who'd be saddle sore and exhausted from all the fresh air that their city lungs weren't accustomed to.

'Penny for them?'

Jake's familiar voice was a welcome distraction from her thoughts. 'Hey, where ya been?'

'Oh, you know. Places to go, people to haunt,' he said evasively. Hallie hated it when he avoided answering questions. He knew everything about her life but she knew nothing about his, or rather his afterlife.

'I'm not in the mood for jokes, Jake,' she said, rubbing her eyes. If he was gonna be in this mood he could just get lost again.

'I can see that, baby,' he said, as she felt his soothing touch on her neck. 'What's up?'

She shook her head, wondering how you started a conversation with your dead husband about how, for the first time since you met him, you wanted to have sex with another man. In all the years they'd been together she had never so much as looked at anybody else. Wanting Aiden so badly was a new and frightening experience.

'Here, let me take your mind off things,' he said, making her breath catch as his hand slipped from her neck, down over her collarbone and onto her breast. 'I love it when your nipples get instantly hard like that.'

Hallie swelled at his touch, her earlier heat only dormant, waiting to be rekindled. Her lips tingled as she sensed his kisses, and she buried her hands in the soft upholstery of the sofa, wishing she could run them over something human, something tangible.

'Damn you, Jake. Why did you have to die?' She hadn't meant to say the words out loud.

He laughed. 'Can't say I was too happy about it myself.' Hallie smiled. His humor always chased away her blues. 'Are you planning to keep your clothes on? You know I can't feel you through them.'

'Sorry.' Hallie disrobed, reclining across the bed to wait for his touch.

She felt his breath on her abdomen. 'Open your legs for me, baby. God, you are so wet,' he rasped, as his finger trailed down through her curls. 'Has my bad girl been horny today?'

Her heart skipped a beat, wondering if he knew. The first flick of his tongue let her know he'd forgotten the question, choosing instead to focus on teasing her clit. Hallie arched in response, throwing her head back and groaning deep in her throat.

Adapting to the new way they made love had meant Hallie always let Jake take the lead, assuming he knew best what would make the experience a good one for him. But she couldn't this time. She was so hot and wet that her mind could focus on nothing other than easing the tension she'd been carrying around all day. Placing a hand on her pussy, she plunged two fingers inside, gasping at the sensation. Her muscles quivered as she pushed at them repeatedly. Her other hand grasped a breast firmly, squeezing her nipple as she felt herself begin to come.

'My God, you're on fire,' she heard Jake say against her skin as he continued lathing her clit with his tongue.

The coils of heat spiraling through her abdomen moved down through her vagina, drawing her body inwards as the first pulses of her orgasm began. More intense than anything she had ever known, the sensation made her pant ragged, broken words that she could barely hear.

'Aiden...fuck me, Aiden,' she cried, head flailing wildly as she reached her peak.

She heard Jake chuckle from his place between her thighs as he continued to caress her. Hallie couldn't usually bear to be touched so intimately after her climax but tonight was different. His tongue brought her back to orgasm in what seemed like seconds. The feeling was less intense, but deeper this time, and she felt her muscles contracting heavily as she gave herself over to the sensation.

Collapsing in a heap when the waves of pleasure began to subside, Hallie found her throat raw. 'Wow, ' she husked. 'What the fuck did you just do to me?'

He ran a hand over her hair, letting her know he was beside her. 'I'd love to take the credit, darlin', but it wasn't me that got you off like that.'

'What do you mean?'

Jake laughed. 'I mean, you were hot for somebody else. I was just filling in for him.'

'Why are you saying that?' Hallie was shocked. How did he know?

'Who is Aiden?'

'Aiden?' Her heart slammed into her chest.

'That's the name you yelled while you were coming so hard.' She could hear the smile in his voice. Jake didn't seem to be angry. 'Whoever he is, he sure got you hot.'

Hallie didn't know what to say. Fuck. She didn't realize she'd called out any name, never mind that one. 'He's nobody.'

'Hardly a nobody if he can make you that horny,' he drawled. 'Come on, 'fess up. Who is he?'

'One of the guests,' she said quietly.

'Is he handsome?'

'Yeah, kinda. I don't want to talk about this Jake.' Hallie got up to put on a nightshirt, suddenly feeling exposed in front of eyes she could not see.

'Do you want to fuck him?'

'Jake!'

'Don't be so shocked. It was bound to happen. You can't spend the rest of your life waiting for me.'

Tears pricked her eyes. Why was he talking about this? 'I don't want anything to come between us.'

'Nothing can separate us, Hallie. Not ever. If the time comes when I can't be here anymore, I will still be in your heart.'

Fear gripped at her chest. 'Are you leaving?'

'Not yet, but you need to realize it's gonna happen one day, when I finally figure out what it is I am here for.'

'Well, I'll deal with that when I have to,' Hallie said stubbornly, not liking the turn the conversation was taking.

'Why don't you invite him up, let me meet him, so to speak?' Jake said, in a tone she could match to an expression in her mind, the one he usually wore when he tried to outsmart her. It didn't work while he was alive, and it wouldn't work now.

'You want to meet him? And that's all, huh?'

'Well...'

'Forget it. That's not going to happen.' He'd nagged her for years to take part in a threesome. She knew it had always been his greatest fantasy.

'Come on, Hallie,' he wheedled. 'He won't even know I am here.'

'Which is exactly the reason we can't do it. It would be wrong. And besides, he's interested in someone else.'

'That's even better. No chance of him falling in love and causing complications,' Jake insisted. 'It would just be a bit of harmless fun with a beautiful woman.'

'And a horny spirit?' Hallie laughed, trying to distract him. She dare not tell him the idea appealed to her greatly. The thought of Jake caressing and stroking her as Aiden fucked her senseless made her insides quiver. But she couldn't do it.

'Just get him in the room. I will do the rest,' he promised, taking her silence as agreement.

'Like I said, it ain't gonna happen.'

Jake's attitude started to bug her the more she thought about it. Later, as she tried to sleep, unsure if he was still with her or not, she said out loud the question that had been churning in her mind. 'Don't you love me anymore?'

His voice came from the other side of the room, as if he was sitting in the rocking chair. 'I'll love you forever. Nothing can change that. Why do you ask?'

'You just seem awful keen to push me towards another man,' she said.

'Sex is one thing. Love is another. I can't give you what you need—what I long to give you—and I want you to be fulfilled.' His sexy chuckle drifted over to her ears. 'And you know how crazy hot the thought of watching you with another guy makes me. But that's all he can have. We can share your body for a night but he can't have your love.'

His words made her uneasy. She didn't like the possessive tone in his voice but she guessed she was all he had now. Could people even find a new love after death?

'So you're thinking about it,' he said, voice hopeful.

'Goodnight Jake.' Her tone told him he was beginning to piss her off. Jake laughed anyway.

'Goodnight, Hallie.'

Chapter 8

Hallie's eyes creaked open the following morning, and she was reluctant to get out of bed. The thought of facing Aiden sent her back under the covers before a nagging voice reminded her of how much she had to do, forcing her to get up.

She needn't have worried. She had a legitimate reason to avoid everyone at breakfast. Cookie seemed much better but wouldn't be able to work for a few days. Hallie stroked her spotted head, sighing at the thought of what the quiet old horse had witnessed the day before.

'You won't tell anyone, will you, girl?' she whispered into Cookie's ear. 'We wouldn't want people to know your owner is a wanton hussy.' Hallie laughed at the expression on the animal's face. Cookie nuzzled her hand looking for more sugar, snorting in disgust when she found it empty.

By the time she could find no other reason to stay away from the house, she discovered that Aiden and the other guests had taken advantage of the chance to join TJ on his trip into town for supplies. The only item on the itinerary for the third day of their stay was country dancing in a local saloon later that evening. The revelers were encouraged to dress in the style of the Old West and the store TJ would take them to in a neighboring town could provide their costumes at a reasonable rate.

Hallie's outfit was one she'd purchased a few months back. The saloon girl costume was pretty typical—purple dress, feathered headpiece, lace garter and fingerless, long gloves. She usually got a buzz out of wearing it, enjoying the chance to feel sexy without her jeans and work clothes. The thought of the reaction she could get when Aiden saw her in it made her insides tremble.

That was if he still intended to speak to her. She'd treated him badly. Hallie owed him a huge thank you for his help with Cookie. The fact she'd lost control wasn't entirely his fault and didn't excuse her behavior. Still, she scurried away when she saw the minivan returning later that afternoon, not yet ready to face him.

'Where have you been, Chica?' Maria asked as Hallie turned up to help with the preparation for dinner. 'I've barely seen you since yesterday.'

'Avoiding the guests,' Hallie said with a wry grin.

'Why would you do that?'

'Hmmm, I wonder why,' she teased.

Maria punched the dough she was working on, refusing to look her in the eye. 'If you don't know then I'm sure I don't either,' she blustered.

Hallie didn't want to make her feel bad. 'Look, just don't tell him anything else, ok?'

'He asked me about you. It wasn't my fault this time.'

'What do you mean he asked? Asked what?'

Maria shrugged. 'If there was a man around and how long you'd had this place.'

'When did this happen?'

'On the first afternoon, just after he arrived.' Maria smiled, always the hopeless romantic no matter what the circumstances. 'He likes you, Hallie.'

'He barely knows me,' she protested.

'Ah, the heart knows what the heart wants.' Maria chuckled, putting her hands up in mock surrender when threatened to stop talking that way or else, by an only slightly joking Hallie, brandishing a dangerous looking carrot.

Dinner time came around too soon, leaving Hallie without an excuse to avoid Aiden further. TJ and Maria couldn't cope alone, and she would have to help them serve the meals. The wood paneled dining room was full when she pushed her way through the swing doors, plates in hand.

Aiden had sat at the table nearest the door with the ever present Kelly at his side and Milton and Rita opposite. Realizing there was just no way to avoid him without letting the whole group know, she stopped to give them their meals first. 'Have you guys had a good day?' she asked brightly, wishing she'd stayed hidden when she saw the slightly pissed look in Aiden's eyes.

'Oh yes, we did,' Kelly gushed, draping her arm through Aiden's. 'I got the best costume for tonight. It matches yours, doesn't it, honey?'

'If you say so,' he answered less than charitably, as he retrieved his arm. 'There wasn't much choice to be honest. There are only so many costumes a guy can wear and still keep his pride.' He laughed, relaxing a little. Hallie would bet the farm on who chose their outfit first but didn't say anything, relieved simply to be having a civil conversation despite the fact her heart was pounding.

'Milton and I are going as Annie Oakley and Wild Bill Hickock,' Rita giggled, 'but Milton looks more like Colonel Sanders in the beard they gave him.'

'Rita looks lovely in her costume,' Milton said, turning up the charm at every opportunity. The object of his affection put a hand on his arm, giving it a gentle squeeze in thanks for the compliment. Hallie smiled at them indulgently, before turning to find Aiden watching her every move.

His gaze flicked down to her breasts, and she knew by the half grin he gave himself before capturing her eyes again that he'd been thinking about the previous afternoon. She swallowed hard, unable to turn away as he blew out a gentle breath through parted lips.

'Uh, thanks for your help yesterday,' she said in a rush. Hallie hadn't intended to speak to him about it in public but she was too much of a wimp to miss the opportunity to get it out of the way with others around her, breaking the tension. 'The vet said Cookie will be ok in a couple of days.'

'I know. I was there when she arrived. Surprised you weren't though.'

Hallie bristled. 'It gets pretty busy around here. Besides, TJ is great with the horses, and I trust him.' She held his gaze, pissed that he dared to judge her based on the short amount of time he had spent on the ranch. Aiden stared back without apology, looking like he wanted to say more. Hallie didn't need to guess if he was still annoyed.

'I meant to apologize again,' Kelly said, sounding sincere. 'I'm so glad she didn't get badly hurt. I just feel awful that I may have done something to cause it.'

'Horses can get spooked by all sorts of things. There is no way of telling when it's going to happen,' Hallie said, glad of the chance to ensure Kelly didn't feel too bad. Aiden had been wrong to blame her so quickly.

'You were mean to me yesterday.' Kelly pouted, turning towards Aiden. 'There was no need to shout at me.'

'I apologized last night. I just have a thing about animals. I hate to see them injured.'

Hallie excused herself, brain racing. So Aiden had spent the evening with Kelly. The lowlife, sleaze bag, son of a bitch had struck out with her, so he wasted no time in going for the sure thing?

She slammed her way back into the kitchen, warning Maria with a raised hand not to ask what the problem was. Truthfully, she didn't know herself. Why did the idea of Aiden doing exactly what he'd come for—finding a woman—annoy her so much?

Chapter 9

The lace on Hallie's dress began to itch. The costume she usually loved so much, the one that made her feel sexy and feminine, had begun to irritate. She felt like she was wearing a sackcloth and ashes rather than purple silk.

Still, the guests seemed to be enjoying themselves. Even Jenny took part in the dance class the organizer always ran before the party got started. A few glasses of wine back at the ranch had loosened them up, and the bar in the venue was doing a good job of keeping them that way.

Hallie allowed her eyes to wander over Aiden again, as if indulging herself was some kind of reward for managing to look away for five minutes. She'd begun to hate him. Not so much for anything he had done, more for the way he made her feel and her helpless attraction to him.

The outfit he'd chosen wasn't helping. Pale buckskin clung to every inch of his legs and ass, making him appear almost naked from a distance save for the fringing snaking its way down the seam of the pants. The matching open vest barely covered his massive shoulders. Tied across his pecs with a tiny leather thong, it did nothing but emphasize his washboard abs and strong biceps. He hadn't bothered with the feather headdress or bow and arrow, choosing to add nothing else but the moccasins and an intricate bead choker.

Hallie laughed. He couldn't have looked less like a Native American if he tried. Aiden was the Chippendale version—all blond hair and gleaming skin. Due to his height, the pants barely fit him; riding so low they exposed most of his heavenly V, her name for the pelvic creases on his lower abdomen. A thin dusting of dark blond hair started just under his navel, trailing downwards as it lead to the Promised Land, before disappearing into a bulging package wrapped in strained leather.

Hallie looked away again. A girl could only take so much. She knocked back the tequila in her hand way too fast, but the heat it caused inside her was still a welcome relief from the one burning in her groin. Damn him. How dare he look so good when she was still so mad at him?

The little Pocahontas with him wasn't helping either. Kelly looked almost as ravishing as the half-naked buck beside her. The fringed mini dress made of suede, with lots of pretty bead embellishments, was beautiful and suited her curvy figure and long dark hair perfectly. Kelly had not shown as much restraint as Aiden when it came to accessories, overdoing it a little with the feathers, poking up at a comical angle at the back of her head, where a leather headband held them in place. She'd gone crazy with the fake tan as well, ending up a weird shade of orange, but it didn't stop her looking fabulous.

Hallie turned her attention to the less frustratingly beautiful party goers. Richard and Mark were comic cowboys, going for giant hats and stupidly large moustaches and fur chaps. Felicity had chosen a frontier dress, *Little House on the Prairie* style, including bonnet. Sharon and Jenny had chosen saloon girl outfits of the same sort as Hallie's. Milton did indeed look like Colonel Sanders despite the elaborate fringing on his jacket that swirled every time he moved. Rita was cute in a jaunty hat and cowgirl skirt, and took great delight in pointing her fake guns at every new person she met. It didn't surprise anyone to find Ike had chosen to dress as a sheriff.

'You gonna join us, Hallie?' Ike bellowed across the room, as he stumbled again over one of the dance moves. His partner, Felicity, winced at the sound then slapped him on the arm as he trod on her foot. God only knew why but they seemed to be hitting it off, Hallie realized. As much as Felicity chastised Ike, the woman seemed to adore him, gazing at him in infatuation during unguarded moments.

'I'll dance with you later, honey,' Hallie replied. She long ago learned all the routines, and preferred to spend the time sitting quietly, watching the revelers. The music ended a few minutes later, allowing the guests time to get a drink and cool down a little before the party got into full swing.

She had every intention of staying on her stool, getting quietly drunk until it was time to go home. Hallie didn't feel like partying. She had one thing on her mind, or rather one man, and she felt sick with longing as she watched him having fun. Guilt, desire and anger warred for dominance in her mind. In spite of his earlier mood, Aiden seemed unaffected by what had passed between them the day before, and she was mad that she couldn't brush it aside so easily.

An hour later, she still hadn't moved from her spot at the bar. A couple of beers had done nothing to improve her mood, so she stopped drinking, aware that she had to stay available should her guests need anything. Looking around to see where they were, she almost smacked her nose into the chest of a man who'd been about to tap her shoulder.

The bar was also open to the public and had begun to get busy. Many locals frequented the venue, especially on a party night. The man who'd been about to disturb her was one she had encountered, and consequently avoided, many times before. Hallie struggled to remember his name. Alan?

'Hi, do you remember me?' he slurred into her face. He stank of whisky as his breath washed over her. Hallie pressed her back against the bar, trying to put some distance between them. Alan placed a hand either side of her chair, trapping her in the circle of his arms.

Hoping her best chance of shortening the encounter was to plead ignorance, Hallie shook her head. 'Not really.'

'Come on now. Don't tell me you've forgotten me already.' Alan looped a finger through one of her curls, allowing his hand to brush against the skin on her neck. 'You were all over me last time we met.'

'If you call sharing a brief conversation as being 'all over you', then you are drunker than you seem,' she said beginning to stand. Hallie had never encouraged his attention. The guy was an arrogant prick.

'You're an uppity bitch, aren't you?' he snarled, pushing her back down onto her seat with a less than gentle hand on her shoulder.

Hallie reeled back and slapped the smirk from his drunken face before cowering in fear as he lifted a hand as if to strike her back. She covered her head, bracing herself for a blow that never came. Peering through a gap in her fingers, she found the space in front of her empty.

A commotion off to her left brought her to her feet to find Aiden standing over the body of the near unconscious Alan. 'Get up, you worthless piece of crap,' Aiden shouted into his face. 'Why don't you try pushing me around?'

Alan wisely chose to stay on the floor, giving Aiden a baleful look as he rubbed the sore spot on his face where he'd been slugged. Ike charged into the fray moments later, keen to back up his buddy and looking for someone else to hit.

'It's over now, Ike,' Aiden said, patting the Marine on the shoulder as if apologizing for keeping all the fun to himself. Ike seemed reluctant to step down, intimidating everyone around him with a stare. Hallie could tell he was just dying for somebody to make a move.

The bartender threw Alan out, apologizing to Hallie and offering her group a drink on him. 'My guess is he doesn't want to lose his best customer,' Felicity drawled, making Hallie smile as she put a comforting arm around her. 'You ok?'

'I'm fine,' she said, not only to Felicity. Her charges were all standing around her uncertainly, scanning her face in concern. 'It was no big deal. Really.'

'Didn't look like no big deal,' Aiden interrupted, face still taut with anger. 'That guy was about to hit you.'

'I handled it,' she said, unable to simply thank him for saving her.

'Yeah, I could see that,' he snapped, green eyes flashing as he came to stand only inches away. 'You know, Hallie. It wouldn't hurt you to be a little more grateful.'

How dare he tell her how to behave? 'Grateful?' she shouted.

'You heard me. This is the second time in as many days that I stepped in and helped you out.'

Hallie realized he was right. For some reason, she lost her manners when Aiden was around. 'Sorry,' she said quietly, placing a hand on his forearm, genuine embarrassment making her cheeks burn.

Aiden's expression softened immediately. 'I don't need an apology. I just want you to stop being mad at me.' He laughed, making her smile. His gaze flicked down to where she touched him. When his eyes met hers again, the expression in them made Hallie want to snatch her hand away, appalled by how rapidly any contact between them became sexual.

She looked around for the others, finding they had made their way back to the dance floor. Even Kelly had forgotten her obsession with Aiden when a Shania Twain track came blaring through the speakers, bringing the crowd to its feet.

'Let me buy you a drink,' she offered, shouting over the noise. He nodded, pointing at a chill cabinet behind the bar filled with bottles of beer before gesturing that he would wait outside.

'Great, more time alone together,' she said under her breath, waving Aiden away innocently when he seemed to think she was talking to him. Minutes later, she stepped through the exit, bottles in hand.

'I'm here,' she heard close behind her, turning to find herself almost right under his nose.

'Oh,' she said, staggering back in surprise. Aiden's hands flew to her waist, steadying her. 'Thanks.' She smiled, squirming as she waited for him to move. But he didn't.

Hallie was close enough to see his nostrils flaring slightly as he took deep, measured breaths. Aiden looked down at her, eyes raking her face before dropping briefly to her cleavage.

'That dress has been driving me crazy,' he said quietly, voice sounding hoarse.

She didn't speak and didn't fight him as he began to pull her body closer to his. Bottles still in her grasp, she had no choice but to allow his large hands to span her waist, thumbs brushing the underside of her corseted breasts.

'Aiden,' she said uncertainly, 'what about Kelly?'

'Shhh,' he whispered, lowering his head as he got her body where he wanted it, pressed hard against his. 'Shut up so I can kiss you, Hallie.'

She held her breath as his mouth seemed to take an age to find hers. The first touch of his lips made her sigh his name, the longing of the last few days making her lose control. Hallie leaned into him, trying desperately to deepen the kiss without the benefit of her hands. Aiden backed up as she surged forward, arms still around her torso, until the wall blocked his progress as they slammed into it.

The ridge of his erection pressed against her abdomen as his hands slid down to her ass, forcing her to grind against him. Aiden ripped his mouth from hers, straining to see the skin he exposed as he slid her dress up her thighs. The breeze tickled her butt as he filled his hands with her flesh, kneading it as he began to thrust towards her gently. His lips found curve of her shoulder, and he kissed it hotly before grazing his teeth over her.

She groaned, melting into him, not noticing as the bottle began to slip from her hand. A loud thud as it hit the ground made them jump.

Cold beer splashed against her leg, distracting Hallie just long enough to give her time to think about what she was doing. Stepping away from him quickly, her hand went to her hair as she attempted to pull herself together.

'I'm sorry…I just can't,' she said in explanation as he asked what was wrong.

The look of confusion on Aiden's face morphed into one of defeat, and he allowed his head to fall back, banging gently against the wall in frustration. His chest heaved from his ragged breathing, and Hallie succumbed to the urge to stare at him a while longer, glorious in his state of arousal, legs spread as he leaned his weight into the wall, hard cock threatening to burst through the laces of his buckskin pants.

He stood abruptly and closed the distance between them, standing mere inches away from her. 'What is your problem?'

'It's complicated,' she said, unable to meet his gaze.

'Yeah, you told me that already.' He snatched the beer from her hand, draining the bottle before slamming it down onto a table and walking towards the road.

'Where are you going?' she shouted.

'Back to the ranch.'

'But it's at least five miles!'

He stopped, sighing as he put his hands on his hips before turning to her. 'Well, I can hardly go back in there like this,' he said, gesturing to a very obviously aroused penis, still begging for release. Hallie shook her head.

'But you'll get lost,' she shouted as he continued on his way.

'Don't worry about me, I'm a country boy,' he said, sounding calm despite what had just happened. 'I'll find my way.'

The urge to follow him began to make her feet move just as the door of the bar flew open, and a blast of noise, heat and light made her turn back.

'Where's Aiden?' Kelly said, eyeing Hallie suspiciously.

'Walking home,' Hallie smiled, deciding fate was trying to tell her something. 'He only just left. You can catch him if you run.'

Chapter 10

'Jake! Where the fuck are you when I need you?' Hallie groaned, ten minutes after she'd stormed into her bedroom. She'd stripped instantly in the soft light from the lamp by her bed, hoping that her nakedness would bring Jake out of hiding but so far there'd been no sign of him. She scanned the room pointlessly, knowing she couldn't see him even if he was there.

'I'm here. I've been watching you,' she heard him say. 'You sure got yourself worked up. What's wrong?'

'Nothing, Jake. I just need you tonight, that's all.'

He laughed. 'How's Aiden?'

Damn. Why had she ever told him about the man who was beginning to drive her crazy? 'I don't know. Anyway, why are you talking about him?'

'Because I know you want him,' Jake said without anger. 'I know what my wife looks like when she's turned on, and, as I know damn well I didn't get you that hot, it had to be him.'

Hallie didn't answer. Truthfully, she had no idea if Aiden had even made it back to the ranch yet. She'd scanned the dark roads and fields as the minivan made its way back to Sleepy Hills but there'd been no sign of him. She didn't trust herself to simply go to his room and check he was in, and she didn't want him getting the wrong idea about why she'd visited if he was there.

'I need you, Jake, don't make me wait any longer,' she pleaded, laying back on top of the bed with her legs apart, trying to tempt him in a way that always worked when he'd been alive.

'You know what you need, Hallie,' he answered, still refusing to touch her. 'You need to be fucked. Hard.'

'Don't tease me.'

'And I want to watch,' he said, ignoring her plea. His voice became dark, and she could picture the look on his face. 'I want to feel your arousal and hear you scream as you come. Your pleasure is my pleasure.'

She knew he meant it in more ways than one. His presence was only possible through his connection to her and anything she felt, he did too. Jake couldn't read her thoughts but he could feel her energy, often knowing before she did how she felt about something. This meant he knew that the thought of having them both had just caused a gush of wetness to seep out of her.

'Why are you fighting it?' His mouth was near her ear, and she felt the first blessed touch of his hand against her throbbing clit. She tried to increase the contact, make him touch her harder, but he resisted. Slow, gentle caresses were not what she needed right then.

'Jake. Please,' she near cried, burning so badly it almost hurt to be denied.

'Soon, Hallie. Soon.'

What the fuck did he mean 'soon'? She wanted him now. About to lose her temper if he continued to play games, she forgot all about it when a loud knock on her door brought her to her feet guiltily.

Shit! Who was it? Had they heard her moaning and begging?

'Just in time,' Jake drawled cryptically.

'What do you mean?' she whispered furiously as she pulled on a robe.

'Open the door and find out.'

Hallie's stomach hit the floor. Jake knew who was on the other side of her door, which meant she did too.

'Hi,' she said nervously as she found Aiden waiting in the hall. He looked as if he'd only just got back to the ranch. His skin gleamed with sweat ,and he seemed slightly breathless.

'Let me in,' he said, jaw tight. His expression left no room for argument, and he gave her only a second to make her mind up before doing it for her, brushing passed.

'You shouldn't be here,' she said, clutching her robe tighter.

'I think it's exactly where I should be,' Aiden said, eyes burning into her. 'And you know it.'

He began to pace in front of her, gearing himself to say something, but then he stopped moving, appearing to notice her properly for the first time.

'Have you been having sex?' he asked quietly, allowing his gaze to take in her mussed hair and flushed face.

Hallie blushed. 'How could I have been? Do you see anybody here?'

Aiden laughed. 'Don't tell me you never touch yourself when you're alone.' His eyes darkened. 'Were you, Hallie? Touching yourself and thinking about me?'

She closed her eyes, shame and want making her heart pound hard as her pussy convulsed at his words and the sound of his voice.

'He wants you so bad, ,' Jake said from somewhere behind her. 'You want him too, don't you?'

She checked to see if Aiden had heard Jake but he was still looking at her with a mixture of lust and anger, like he wanted to either fuck her or throttle her.

Jake laughed silkily in her ear. 'I think you know what's going to happen.' Hallie shook her head mutely, unable to answer him with Aiden looking at her.

'Stop fighting it,' Aiden said, misunderstanding the reason for her action.

'Yeah, stop fighting,' Jake said, sliding an unseen hand between her buttocks. Hallie took a step forwards, trying to escape his caress but he moved with her, using the opportunity to slide a finger over her clit.

Hallie's breath caught in her throat as a spasm of electricity went through her. Sinking her teeth into her lip to stop from crying out, she could do no more than stare helplessly at Aiden as he watched her.

'Fuck, Hallie. Don't look at me like that,' he gasped, 'unless you are willing to give me what your eyes are promising.'

'Oh, she's willing.' Jake laughed into her ear. 'Aren't you, baby?' His hands had moved and were at that very moment sliding up the front of her torso to cup her breasts, tweaking the nipples almost painfully before moving away. He left her alone briefly, allowing her time to suck in a ragged breath and try to clear her head. The reprieve didn't last long. The next thing she felt was the flick of his tongue as he parted the lips of her pussy and began to tease her clit.

'You want me,' Aiden said, walking towards her as he began to unlace the buckskin trousers of the outfit he still wore. 'Don't bother denying it. I can see it in your face.' He stopped speaking as he freed his long hard penis, sliding the leather down his legs and kicking the pants away. The vest followed instantly, leaving him before her totally naked and highly aroused.

Hallie wanted to sink to her knees and take his cock in her mouth but she still couldn't move, couldn't be the one who started it.

'Can you imagine how it would feel?' Jake asked, standing behind her again. 'How it would taste?

Aiden stared at her. 'You're shaking, Hallie. Are you afraid of me?'

She shook her head. Aiden couldn't know that Jake's touch had made her so weak that the sight of his body, hard and hot for her, made her feel faint. Her knees were threatening to buckle beneath her if the torture didn't stop.

Jake plunged two fingers between her legs, moving them rapidly over her flesh. 'Tell him what you want.'

Aiden took another step forward, reaching out a hand and stroking her cheek as she watched him helplessly. Hallie couldn't see him clearly through her lust-glazed eyes. She heard her own breath coming in restrained gasps.

'Tell me what you want,' Aiden said. 'You are so hot for me I could take you right now, but you gotta ask for it.'

'Tell him,' Jake urged, adding a finger to the ones already making her cream all over his hand.

'What do you want?' Aiden asked again, putting a strong hand at the back of her neck, forcing her to stare into his eyes. 'Tell me.'

Chapter 11

'Fuck me,' she whispered, voice weak as Jake's free hand urged her to slip off her robe, allowing it to fall to the floor at her feet. 'I want you to fuck me.'

She heard Aiden's sigh of relief. The hand on her neck tightened, and he forced her body against his, searing her mouth with a kiss. Hallie surged forward, wrapping her arms around him, loving the feel of his skin beneath her hands.

Aiden picked her up, placing her roughly on the bed before lying down beside her. She knew he intended to kiss and caress her a little, trying to make it good for her, but it wasn't what she wanted. Jake knew it too. 'Suck his cock,' he ordered, taking her nipple into his mouth.

Hallie reached over to straddle Aiden, kissing his mouth hungrily before dragging her lips away to trail them down his neck. She could taste the sweat on his skin as she grazed her teeth over his flesh. Aiden groaned in response, his breathing getting hoarse as her mouth continued its journey down his body and over his nipples, tongue dipping into his navel briefly before finding its way to the head of his dick. She moved to kneel between the V of his thighs, stroking him for a moment before dipping her head.

'Hallie,' he moaned at the first gentle touch of her lips. 'Ah, fuck,' he said, as she opened her mouth wide, taking him right to the back of her throat.

'You look so good, baby,' Jake rasped, parting the cheeks of her ass, encouraging her to open her legs, allowing him room to lick at her pussy. Hallie growled at his touch, sucking harder and faster on

Aiden as Jake drove her crazy with his mouth. Her nails sank into the skin of Aiden's thighs, causing him to hiss in response.

'Stop, Hallie. Please,' he begged on a throaty laugh. 'I can't take much more of that. I want to be inside you.'

'So do I,' Jake said. 'Get the vibrator.'

Damn. What was she going to do? She didn't want Jake to feel left out but she had no intention of making Aiden feel inadequate by pulling out a sex aid while he was trying to make love to her.

'I can't do it with the light on,' she said, thinking fast and hoping that her answer was vague enough to make sense to both of them.

Aiden laughed indulgently as she reached over him to flick off the lamp, taking the opportunity to suck a hard nipple into his mouth when her breast rubbed his cheek. Hallie sat on him, spreading her legs as she held his cock at her opening. She bit her lip as the first hard inch or two forced its way into her swollen wetness. The feeling took her breath away, days of want and months of loneliness combining to make the sensation a bittersweet one.

'Does that feel good?' Jake asked beside her. Hallie nodded, unable to speak regardless of the fact she couldn't in front of Aiden. 'Take him deeper,' Jake ordered, his hands pushing down on her shoulders.

Her thighs shook as Aiden's hands gripped her hips, forcing her further onto his prick, doing Jake's bidding without knowing it. 'Oh my God, you are so fucking tight and wet,' Aiden gasped as her ass met his hips, her body totally impaled on him.

Jake's hands at her shoulders urged her forwards to lie over Aiden's body as she took his first thrusts. Aiden's hands split her ass, holding her legs wide as he plunged in and out of her vagina, jerking her body with the force.

'Get the thing, Hallie,' Jake begged. 'I can't wait much longer.'

She kissed Aiden, making sure he couldn't follow the movements of her hand as she reached under the pillow to grab the toy, moving her hand out of his vision as soon as she had it. She pinned Aiden to the mattress with her weight, sucking at his neck for a moment, just long enough to put the slender tip of the vibrator inside her ass.

'Oh, that's it baby. That's it,' Jake groaned, pushing against the shiny metal toy, urging it gently inside her. She hoped he had the sense not to turn it on.

Hallie's pussy began to quiver in response to the extra stimulus, and she groaned loudly against Aiden's chest where her head lay. He heard the change in her tone and adjusted position, bringing his feet up and bending his knees to spread her wider as he held her hips and began to fuck her furiously.

'Yes,' Jake gasped as Hallie was forced upright over Aiden by his thrusts. The toy stayed where Jake had put it, leaving his hands free to reach around from behind and grab her breasts. His movements matched hers, and she felt his mouth against her ear as he told her he was about to explode.

'That's it, baby,' Aiden rasped as her pussy began to spasm around his dick. 'Come for me, Hallie.'

She began to do just that, bracing her hands on his chest, digging in her nails as she began to jerk frantically. 'Fuck,' she screamed as a spasm rocketed through her pussy and ass at the same time, clenching and releasing both the vibrator and Aiden's huge penis.

Jake's hands got painful on her breasts, and she heard his orgasm begin, his breath hot and hard on her neck. 'Fuck me, Aiden,' she cried, desperate for him to be a part of what was happening to her.

Below her, Aiden joined them both, his body beginning to jerk up into her as he felt the pulsating walls of her pussy sucking at him. 'Hallie,' he groaned, reaching up to drag her face down to his as the shudders racked through him, breathing his words into her open, gasping mouth. 'So good...so fucking good.'

Hallie heard the cries of the two men combining with hers, and she began to come again almost as soon as her first peak ended. Aiden and Jake continued to stroke her as their own orgasms waned, both of them whispering words of encouragement as she shuddered to a breathless, exhausting halt.

As soon as she could move, Hallie fell off of Aiden, wrapping the sheet around her to dispose of the vibrator without him seeing. His arm went around her shoulder immediately, dragging her body back to his.

Finally, the sounds of their ragged breathing subsided, leaving them holding each other quietly in the darkness of the night.

'Wow that was amazing!' Jake said, his incredulous laugh making her start. She'd forgotten he was there and, by the sounds of it, lying right beside her.

Aiden got her attention by pulling her closer for a lingering kiss. 'I don't get you, ' he said.

'What don't you get?'

'Why would you fight me so hard when you knew how hot it could be between us?' His words could have been considered arrogant but Hallie knew he had every reason to believe what he was saying based on her reaction to him, so she let it ride. 'If you tell me again that it's complicated, I'm gonna slap your bare ass,' he threatened, laughing.

She giggled. 'Well it is,' she said, voice getting serious. 'You have no idea. Look, Aiden, there's something you should know.'

'Don't tell him,' Jake shouted. 'He won't understand.'

'What is it?' Aiden said.

'Forget it.' God! She was getting pretty sick and tired of juggling two conversations.

'Tell me,' he urged. She shook her head. 'Ok, but don't blame me if I refuse to let your little secrets get in our way.'

'They're not gonna get in our way, because this is not going to happen again.'

'Why not?' said Jake.

'Why not?' echoed Aiden.

'Oh, for fuck's sake,' Hallie shouted, leaping to her feet, unable to tell them both to shut up and leave her alone. Wrapping her robe around her, she picked his clothing off the floor, throwing them at him dismissively. 'You'd better go.'

'Jesus,' Aiden said, flopping backwards onto the pillow in frustration. 'What in the hell is wrong now?' Hallie folded her arms, turning away from him to show she had no intention of explaining herself to him.

'You're crazy, you know that, don't you?' Aiden growled, shoving his legs angrily into his pants. Bunching the moccasins and vest in his hand rather than put them on, he strode towards her. 'There's a thin line between crazy and cruel.'

Guilt made her cheeks flame. 'What is that supposed to mean?'

Aiden stepped nearer, breathing into her face as he spoke. 'It means that fucking me and throwing me out before my sweat has even cooled on your skin is a pretty twisted way to treat someone.'

'Wait. Don't go like this,' Hallie said as he stormed from the room, door slamming behind him.

'Don't worry. He'll be back,' she heard behind her.

'Shut up, Jake.'

'Hey, why are you pissed at me?' He laughed, seeming not to care how much turmoil he'd caused by taking advantage of her loyalty to him and playing games with her emotions.

'I just want to be alone now,' she said. Hallie heard him sigh.

'Why are you mad? I thought you'd be happier than this after the best sex of your life.'

'It wasn't my choice. You totally manipulated Aiden and me so you could get your thrill.'

Hallie could hear the anger in his voice. 'What's with this 'Aiden and me' shit?'

'I didn't mean it that way. It came out wrong,' she explained, wondering why she was bothering.

'Are you beginning to have feelings for him?'

So now he thought he had the right to get jealous? 'Just go away. I've had enough,' she said as she rubbed her eyes.

'Don't worry, I'm going,' he shouted. 'I'd hate to get in the way.'

Hallie jumped as the picture she kept over the fire, the one of her and Jake's wedding day, flew off the edge, dropping onto the thick rug. Had Jake made it move?

'Huh!' she said to herself as she picked it up. 'Now when did he learn to do that?'

Chapter 12

Hallie was already pretty sick of men by the time she realized Aiden planned to sulk over what had happened the previous night. The day they were about to be forced to spend together, due to the fact the itinerary had them scheduled to attend a rodeo, would be fraught with tension already, without having to deal with his stony demeanor.

Aiden hid his eyes under his hat every time she turned his way, refusing to look at her dead-on. Hallie thought it was a little rude given the fact he'd gotten what he wanted out of her the night before. Maybe he always got this cold after sex, scared that perhaps the woman would want more than he was ready to give?

She was fortunate in some ways, kept so busy that she didn't have much time to dwell on him once they hit the circuit in Tucson. Tickets, seating, drinks and refreshments took up most of her afternoon. The only time she had to make contact with him was when he sullenly refused anything she offered him.

Kelly wasn't having a much better time of things, Hallie noted. His mood seemed to encompass anyone who got near him. The rest of the guests realized early on in the day that he wasn't in a sociable frame of mind and gave him a wide berth. Kelly, on the other hand, seemed to think that if she just tried harder, she could get him out of his blues.

But she'd given up too by the time Hallie and TJ herded the group into the venue's bar later that evening. The general consensus seemed to be that a great day was had by all. Even Aiden had surfaced from his self imposed isolation long enough to thank Hallie and her staff very formally for organizing the event.

Taken aback by direct eye contact after a day of looking at the top of his hat, it took Hallie a moment to recover. 'Oh, thanks.' She smiled nervously. 'Let me buy you all a beer,' she offered to all, looking directly at Aiden.

'I'll get my own,' he said, turning away with a distant look in his eyes. Go fuck yourself, Hallie thought murderously. She was tired of playing nice. If Aiden knew for one minute what a tortured, sleepless night she'd had due to guilt over what she and Jake had done to him, he wouldn't be so judgmental. Or maybe he would. Who the hell knew?

Thankfully for her, the evening passed quickly. The minivan and its cargo of very tired people pulled back into the ranch a little before midnight, coming to a stop in the bright, moonlit yard.

Waiting by the van's door, she said goodnight to each of the guests as they disembarked. 'Great day,' shouted Ike as he waited for the woman who was the other half of the now inseparable couple they had become. Felicity smiled happily as she took Ike's hand.

'Goodnight, you two,' Hallie said to their retreating backs.

Mark and Jenny came next. Their romance hadn't progressed beyond spending almost all their time together but Hallie sensed the shy couple really liked each other. Hopefully, this week would be enough to set them on the road to something more in the future. Kelly got off behind them, giving Hallie's arm a squeeze as she hobbled back to the house, still wearing her stupid silver mules.

Rita and Milton were next, still blissfully happy. Hallie fully expected to receive a wedding invitation sometime in the months following their departure.

Sharon and Richard got off the van together although they hadn't become an item. They seemed to be partners in crime, putting all their efforts into teasing the others or pairing up automatically so they wouldn't come between the budding romances.

Aiden was the last from the van, stepping around Hallie without acknowledging her. 'Goodnight,' she shouted at his back sarcastically, stunned he could be so rude.

He stopped walking. 'Was it?'

She understood his cryptic answer. 'Yes,' she said earnestly, 'no matter how it ended.'

Aiden seemed to be weighing her words. 'I know I'm gonna regret asking this, but what in the hell happened?'

'I can't tell you. I'm sorry,' she said, knowing she was about to smash the tentative truce between them.

'Does it make you feel good? Playing games with people this way?' Aiden said, anger returning in a flash.

'I wasn't playing games,' she shouted, the day of tension taking its toll. 'If I remember right, you turned up at my door uninvited and of your own free will.'

'Lady, you know why I showed up last night.' His eyes narrowed in the bright moonlight. 'One of us had to find out where this thing between us would lead.'

'What do you mean? It was never gonna lead anywhere.'

'So, it was just sex?'

Hallie didn't understand why he found it so difficult to accept. She thought it was all he wanted from anyone, Kelly included.

'Yes, it was just sex. Like the kind you had a couple nights ago.'

'What?'

'The night you spent with Kelly,' she explained angrily. Why was he acting so dumb? 'You said you'd apologized to her the night after the ride.'

Aiden laughed as he got her drift. 'And you took that to mean I had sex with her?'

'Well, didn't you?'

He shook his head. 'No, I didn't. Is that what this is about? Jealousy?'

'Oh, spare me,' Hallie said, unwilling to let go of the anger that was protecting her from having to confess the truth to him. 'You can fuck who you want, when you want. I don't care.'

'I found that out already,' he said, calmly. He moved closer, forcing Hallie to back up against the side of the minivan to maintain eye contact. 'And to be honest, I don't mind servicing you like some stallion.' He ignored her shocked gasp. 'What I don't get is why you played so hard to get.'

Hallie raised a hand to slap his face but he caught it, pinning it above her head while trapping the other to her side. 'Is that what gets you off?' he asked quietly, mouth dipping as if about to kiss her. 'Was making me want you so bad I can't sleep part of some fucked up game you like to play?'

Aiden crushed her lips with his. Her initial reaction was to struggle and push him away with her body but he held her firm, not allowing her to escape. Within seconds she was straining to increase the pressure of her mouth on his, sighing in disappointment when he lifted his head.

'Sorry, Miss Hallie,' TJ said as he appeared from the other side of the vehicle. 'Do you need me to put the van away?' He looked at his feet, obviously embarrassed to have walked in on something.

Aiden took a step back, turning away to hide the erection that had been pressing into Hallie's abdomen only moments before. Hallie looked at TJ briefly, nodding at him before dropping her head on a sob and running blindly into the fields.

Chapter 13

Aiden found her an hour later, wrapped in a blanket as she sat on the ground, leaning against the side of a stable. She began to get up, unwilling to have another humiliating encounter with him but he stilled her with a raised hand.

'Please, don't run,' he said gently. 'I've come to apologize. I'm sorry, Hallie. You didn't deserve that.'

She sat back down, grudgingly offering him a bit of space on the horse blanket she'd spread on the ground to protect her clothing from the dirt and straw. She'd been thinking about him just before he'd appeared. So there was nothing between him and Kelly? All her assumptions about Aiden had been wrong.

Hallie knew the time she'd spent with him had been amazing and she wasn't surprised that her treatment immediately afterwards had offended him. But he didn't know what she did. She hadn't made love to him alone. He'd benefited from the combined sexual energy of two people – her and Jake. Just thinking about it made her feel guilty.

'TJ is a good kid,' Aiden said as he sat, surprising her with the unexpected topic. 'He just ripped me a new one back there.' He laughed.

'What do you mean?'

Aiden looked sheepish. 'He heard what I said to you and tried to punch me out for it after you ran off. '

'Oh my God, I'm sorry, Aiden,' she said, feeling even guiltier than she did already.

'It's ok. I deserved it.' He laughed.

'You didn't hit him, did you?'

'Hallie, what do you take me for?'

'Sorry, I guess I just assumed you would fight back.'

'Then you have a pretty low opinion of me if you think I would hit a kid.' Aiden laughed after a moment, no longer angry. 'Besides, he was swinging so wildly he wouldn't have been able to hit the side of a barn. I just kept out of his way until he ran out of steam.'

Hallie giggled. 'Poor TJ.'

'He doesn't have all that red hair for nothing. Kid's got a fiery temper when he gets going.' He chuckled.

'So, are you buddies again?' Hallie asked, hoping they were. TJ practically hero worshipped Aiden, hanging on his every word.

'Yes, we got it all straightened out. In fact, he told me a few things.'

Hallie didn't like the sound of that. 'Oh yes?'

'Yes. Like the fact you haven't so much as looked at a man since Jake died. Is that true?'

She nodded. 'That's not so amazing. He's only been gone a year.'

Aiden turned to her. 'Point is I thought there was something special between us. Then last night, you acted so strange at a time when we should have been getting closer after the mind-blowing sex we'd just had, but instead you pushed me away.' He picked at an imaginary speck on his jeans. 'The only thing I could figure is that maybe you had the odd casual affair from time to time and that you didn't care much one way or the other about me.'

'That's not it,' Hallie said, touched by his honesty but afraid of how he would react to her reply. 'There hasn't been anyone else. Please just trust me when I tell you there is a reason things can't go any further.'

'Do you have any feelings for me at all?' he asked, ignoring her reply.

'Yes,' she said quietly, unable to lie over something that seemed to matter to him so much.

'Then why are you pushing me away?'

'Don't keep asking me, Aiden, please,' she begged, voice beginning to crack.

'Ok, ok. Don't get upset. We'll talk about something else.'

He fell quiet, leaning into the wall beside her to stare up at the moonlit mountain in the distance. 'You've got one hell of a view from here,' he said finally.

She nodded. 'It's my favorite place on the ranch. When the moon is out you can see for miles.'

'The light makes your hair look like a halo,' he said, bringing her attention back to him. His fingers trailed through a strand, holding it out to catch the moon rays. Hallie turned to find his eyes on her mouth. Her breath stilled as she saw him run the silky strands through his fingers before twisting the hair around them, using it to gently pull her closer.

He took off his hat, throwing it to the ground as his lips met hers. Hallie knew she should fight him or push him away but she couldn't. Aiden's mouth began to move down towards her neck, sucking and grazing her skin.

He got to his knees and pulled Hallie onto hers. His hands found her denim clad ass, using it to bring her body up against his. One of his thighs pushed between hers, and she felt the first pang of heat course through her.

Aiden began to pull the t-shirt from her body, dropping his head to her pink lace bra as soon as it was exposed. She moaned gently as his mouth wet the fabric covering her nipple where he sucked on it, all the while fumbling with the zipper of her jeans. Hallie felt the cool air on her belly as he pushed them open, sliding the flat of his hands under the fabric at her hips, running his fingers over her skin to knead her buttocks.

Hallie returned the favor, freeing his erection from the confines of his clothing and rubbing the strong shaft between her palms. Aiden pulled her upright, sliding her jeans and panties off before removing his own clothing.

Bathed in moonlight, they embraced, totally naked and connected from head to toe. Hallie's head barely reached his shoulder, and he had to bend to kiss her, letting his hands run up and down her thighs before dipping into the wetness between her legs.

'You know my biggest regret about the last night?' he whispered against her mouth. 'That I didn't get to taste you.'

He pulled her down to the blanket, kissing her mouth before trailing his lips down her body to the pulsing bud waiting for his touch. Hallie held her breath as he flicked his tongue over her clit for the first time then teased it further with heavy, broad strokes. She jerked from the blanket, burying her hands in his hair to keep his mouth against her.

Aiden sucked her flesh between his wet lips, holding it firmly while he swirled his tongue over her again and again. Her legs began to shake, and he pushed them out of the way roughly, groaning as he buried his head further between her thighs. Her ass left the floor all together as she felt a thick finger probing at the entrance of her pussy but he didn't enter her, leaving her to jerk helplessly against him as he held her on the brink.

Hallie looked down to his head, finding him staring up her body, taking in every reaction. Moving to one side, he bit her thigh gently before pushing a frustratingly small amount of his finger further inside her. Hallie started to whimper, urging him to make her come with the writhing of her hips.

Aiden's thumb began to circle her clit and he finally, blessedly, slid in the rest of his finger, probing deeper and deeper with each thrust. His free hand held her thigh against the ground as he lowered his head, brow creased in concentration as he watched her pussy convulsing around him.

Hallie's body arched sharply as her orgasm hit, making her torso leave the blanket. Aiden moved up her body to suck a nipple into his mouth while his hand continued to make her come.

He kissed her as he covered her body again with his own, and Hallie could taste herself on his lips. Aiden nudged her legs further apart, holding her steady as he pushed his cock inside her.

'Ah fuck, Hallie. You are so wet,' he said as he slid further into her. Aiden shifted his weight onto his elbows, placing his forearms either side of her shoulders as he cupped her head in his hands. Hallie urged him further inside by clasping the cheeks of his ass, pushing in time with his slow, measured thrusts.

Being alone with him gave Hallie time to truly experience making love to the man. Her hands made an inventory of every part of his body that was within her reach, from the cords of muscle at the back of his arms to the dimples in the dip of his back. She could feel the springy hairs on his thighs brushing against hers and the small tremors in his abdomen as he pushed into her over and over again.

Hallie struggled to free her hands, wanting to sink them into his hair. Aiden gave her the space to move, taking the opportunity to clutch at a breast, covering the entire thing with his massive hand. His change in position brought his pelvic bone into better contact with hers and she began to feel the tiny electric shocks of arousal spear through her again, making her grind against him. He followed her lead, supporting his body weight on his hands to increase the pressure against her mound.

She surged up to kiss him but he met her halfway, plunging his tongue into her mouth as his thrusting became faster and harder. Hallie put her weight on her elbows, using her body to grind against him as the first warning spasms of her orgasm begun. She fell back as Aiden put an arm under her ass, lifting her pelvis against him and told her he was about to come.

Hallie jerked under him as wave after wave of sensation rocked through her body and into him. Aiden exploded into her as she began to whimper, gritting his teeth as he pummeled her hips. The sound of his hoarse cries washed over her, and she put her arms around him, holding his body as he shuddered to a halt.

She didn't know how long they lay on the blanket, limbs entangled, still joined. Aiden raised his head, kissing her lazily, barely moving his lips over hers as they held each other. Hallie began to feel the cold, pushing him away with her body to turn and find her clothing. She smiled to herself as she saw the few items she had been wearing scattered far and wide.

'Pass my underwear, will you?' she asked him, pointing behind him to the little pink pile at the edge of the blanket. She pulled on her jeans and top, stuffing the items in her pocket when he handed them back.

Aiden lay on his back to wiggle into his jeans, groaning as he closed the zipper over still sensitive flesh. He sat up and crossed his legs, naked from the waist up. 'You're quiet,' he said, watching her eyes for a reaction.

'I've got a lot to think about, Aiden,' was all she would say, unable to confess that she felt like she had just cheated on her husband. The fact he was dead made no difference.

'Aw, Hallie, don't shut me out again.'

'I won't. I promise,' she said, rushing to kiss him. 'Just give me a couple of days to sort out how I feel about this, ok?'

He wasn't satisfied. 'Don't you know how you feel?'

'Yes, I do,' Hallie said, dropping her head as she smiled. 'Problem is I don't know if I'm allowed to.' She could see Aiden wanted to say more, much more, but he seemed to realize there was no point in pushing her.

'I better go back alone,' she confessed as he began to walk alongside her. 'I think we've caused enough gossip for one night, don't you?' She smiled, kissing his cheek as she left him standing alone in the moonlight.

Chapter 14

'You fucked him, didn't you? I can smell him all over you.'

Hallie jumped as she heard Jake's angry voice behind her. She'd barely stepped through the door to her room before the questions began.

'Why are you mad? I thought you wanted me to fuck other guys,' she snapped back, furious at him.

'Jesus, Hallie,' he said. 'When did you get to be such a hard-faced bitch?'

Hallie paused, wanting to find the right words. 'I haven't changed. I'm still the same person. It was you that pushed me to involve Aiden in our lives, and now you have to realize, once you set things in motion, you can't always control where they lead.'

The room went quiet for a very long time. Hallie eventually gave up waiting for a reply and set about getting ready for bed. She knew Jake was still with her somewhere.

Later, as she stared at the ceiling, trying in vain to fall asleep, he finally spoke. 'Are you going to leave me?'

'I don't want to, Jake, but what's happening here can't go on forever. At first, the knowledge you were here kept me strong and got me through those awful months after you died. And I was happy to live like that for a while.'

'And now?'

'Now, I don't think it's good for either of us. I'm stopping you from passing over or whatever it is you call it up there, and you are stopping me from moving on.'

Jake sounded hurt. 'What am I supposed to do? Sit here and watch while you fall in love with someone else? It's not like I can leave.'

'I know. And to be honest, I'm still not ready to let you go.' She sat up, turning in the direction his voice had been coming from. 'All I know is that things are changing, and it's nothing to do with Aiden. He couldn't have gotten close unless I wanted him to.'

'God, I'm an idiot. I can't believe I actually pushed you towards him. All I could think about was how to get you to fulfill one of my fantasies.' Jake laughed bitterly. 'Be careful what you wish for, eh?'

Hallie smiled. 'Look, there is no need to be so sad. I'm not going anywhere.'

'You say that now but what about Aiden?'

She sighed. 'Aiden won't be a problem. He is leaving in two days, and I doubt very much I will ever hear from him again once I tell him the truth.'

'Aw shit, Hallie. How many times do I have to say it? Don't tell him.'

She shook her head. 'I have to. He deserves to know what happened that night.'

'Take my word. He won't thank you for it.'

'I'm sure you are right,' she said. 'But I have no choice. It's just something I have to do.'

Hallie began to get tired but Jake seemed full of questions. She struggled to answer them all as honestly as she could. She owed him that much. Eventually she began to lose patience.

'Look, what happened between us was private. I am not going to give you any details.'

He sounded belligerent. 'It's a simple question. Was he better than me?'

'He wasn't better, just different.'

'Different how?'

'Stop it, Jake.'

'You're still my wife. I got a right to know what you been up to.'

She wished he would just let it go. 'I'm not going over this again. I'm sorry that I ever met him, ok? Is that what you wanted to hear?'

'It's a start,' he said.

'Don't get cocky. I'm not sorry for you. I'm sorry for me.'

'You've got nothing to feel sorry for yourself over,' Jake shouted. 'It's me that is trapped here with nothing to do but wait for you to remember me.'

'You're not the only one that's trapped,' she said, tiredness and his endless questions beginning to make her feel weepy. 'But don't worry. Within a couple of days, things will be back to normal. You'll have me all to yourself again.'

'You make that sound like it's a bad thing,' he said petulantly.

Hallie didn't answer, determined not to talk anymore, at least for that night. She rolled over in bed, turning her back on him. Jake's emotions swung between anger, hurt and curiosity. Hearing him go on and on just compounded her misery.

Having sex with Aiden alone had changed everything. For the first time in years, Hallie had done something just because she wanted to. Maybe needed to. And it felt so good. She'd been foolish to think that the only reason their first sexual encounter had been so mind-blowing was because of Jake's presence. Aiden had just proved to her that, whatever the relationship with her ex-husband, the reaction she'd had that night was all down to him.

Just the thought of him made her hot. She began to get wet as she relived their intense fuck behind the stables. For the first time since Jake's death, Hallie began to resent his presence. Jesus, she couldn't even masturbate in private. Jake's eyes saw everything.

'I know you are thinking of him,' she heard him say. 'You want him right now, don't you?' Hallie ignored him, certain she couldn't take another two hours of interrogation. 'I can help you. Let me help you, Hallie.'

She felt his hand on her thigh as he tried to pull her legs gently apart. 'Jake, please don't.'

'I don't mind, baby. If he gets you this hot, we can all benefit,' he said, voice silky.

Hallie wanted to slap him. Since when had he become more obsessed with having sex with her than respecting her? Maybe Jake's body hadn't been the only thing to die?

Chapter 15

Hallie did everything within her power to avoid Aiden for the whole of the following day. It hadn't been easy.

Thursday's schedule gave the residents a choice of activity—whitewater rafting, fly fishing or individual improver lessons with the horses—and Hallie had prayed Aiden wouldn't pick the latter; the one she was in charge of.

He'd caught her eye at breakfast and she'd barely managed a tight smile as she dashed passed him, gesturing that she was busy. Hallie ignored the slightly bewildered look he'd given her as she disappeared from view.

She'd felt a little guilty sending TJ off alone to take the group rafting without her. If none of the guests wanted the extra lessons, she usually joined her staff for the day, helping them out. This time was different. She needed the space that having Aiden and the rest of them out of the way would give her.

Keeping a low profile until they had gone, Hallie breathed a sigh of relief as the minivan pulled out of the yard. The remainder of her day was spent catching up on paperwork and checking in on Cookie. She avoided spending any time in her bedroom. Still angry at Jake, she wanted nothing to do with him until she and Aiden had spoken. Jake would only try to talk her out of telling him.

The hours dragged on, and Hallie found the butterflies in her stomach intensify as she ran out of excuses to delay the inevitable. Finally, once the ranch was dark and she heard the guests leaving the bar after a couple hours spent drinking and reminiscing about the day, she went to him.

As she approached the door to Aiden's room, Hallie got a strange sense of foreboding. She chased the feeling away, sure it was only nerves making the hairs on the back of her neck rise. Taking a deep breath, she knocked.

Sounds of movement on the other side of the door were followed by hushed whispers, and a woman's voice. 'Who is it?' Aiden shouted, before whispering angrily to the person with him that they should be quiet. Hallie stepped back, panic setting in as she wished she hadn't chosen that precise moment to speak to him. Anger followed by relief that she didn't owe him an explanation about a damn thing set her feet in motion and she turned, about to run away as she heard the door open behind her.

'Hallie?'

She stopped at the sound of Aiden's voice. He was half dressed, jeans open at the waist far enough to show a sprinkling of the hair at his groin.

'I wanted to speak to you,' she said, cheeks burning as she stared at him, 'but it can wait. Sorry I disturbed you.'

Kelly's voice drifted passed him from inside the room. 'Aiden, who is it?'

He dropped his head, running a frustrated hand through his hair before bringing his eyes back to hers. 'I don't suppose it will make any difference if I tell you this isn't what it looks like?'

'You don't owe me any explanations,' she said, turning on her heel.

Hallie ran through the house, slamming into her room breathlessly. She felt like an idiot. Why had she spent the whole day worrying about the feelings of a man who'd proven he wasn't worth it?

Between Aiden and Jake, she was beginning to feel like piece of meat, something to be used at will. Both of them were a waste of emotion as far as she was concerned. Jake seemed to have morphed into a purely sexual being with no capacity for love and Aiden, God only knew what was going through his mind. Why had he chased her so relentlessly if all he'd wanted was an easy lay? Kelly had been willing and available if all he needed was sex.

She jumped as Aiden's voice reached her ears from the other side of the door. 'Hallie, open up.'

'Go away,'

The knocking got louder, making the walls shake. 'Open this door or I swear to God I'll kick it in.'

Who the fuck did he think he was? She stomped over to the door, flinging it open to find Aiden standing there, still in his jeans, a flushed, angry look on his face. 'Stop that. You'll wake the guests.'

'Can I come in?'

Hallie laughed. 'Why? Did Kelly kick you out of bed?'

'We weren't in bed.'

'Only because I disturbed you,' she snapped, turning her back on him.

'Why do you care?' he said, changing tack. 'It's not as if you give a damn.'

'You're right. I don't. Now will you leave?'

Aiden stepped into the room, rattling the walls as he slammed the door. 'No, I am not going anywhere until you give me an explanation for the way you've been acting today.'

'If you think I owe you an explanation after what I just saw, you are stupider than you look,' she said, stunned at his arrogance.

'You saw nothing.'

'I'm sure Kelly will be thrilled to hear herself described in such glowing terms.'

Aiden put his hands on his hips, taking a deep breath before he spoke. 'She came to my room on some stupid excuse. Said I'd called her and asked her to come.'

'Didn't you?'

He laughed. 'No, I didn't. I figured it was some silly idea she'd dreamed up. I was in the process of throwing her out when you showed up.'

'Do you expect me to believe that?' she said angrily. 'How stupid do you think I am?'

'I don't know. How stupid are you?' His voice was harsh. 'Stupid enough to play games with me it seems.'

His words took her by surprise. 'What do you mean?'

'I mean avoiding me all day, refusing to even look at me, then turning up at my door.' He took a step towards her. 'Do we have to go through this every time? Why are you making things so complicated?'

Hallie didn't know how to react. The honesty in his gaze made her feel guilty anew, anger at him and Kelly pushed to one side as she remembered the reason she'd gone to him in the first place.

Aiden took advantage of her silence, grasping her arms in his hands and pulling her against him. 'You want to stay away but you can't. Is that it?' he asked as he lowered his mouth to hers. The kiss deepened while Hallie ignored the voice in her brain reminding her that she needed to talk to him, explain about Jake.

Jake! Was he here, watching somewhere? Hallie leapt from Aiden's arms at the thought. How could she have forgotten him?

'What's wrong?' Aiden said, following her gaze as it darted around the room.

'That,' Hallie said, pointing at the wedding picture on the mantel as it began to slide slowly towards the edge before flying forwards suddenly, towards Aiden's head.

'Fuck,' he shouted, ducking just in time.

Hallie screamed. 'Jake, stop that right now!' She walked around the room, trying to sense where he was. 'I'm still gonna tell him, so you may as well stop whatever it is you think you are doing.'

She turned, finding Aiden staring at her as if she were crazy. 'What's going on and who the fuck is Jake?'

Chapter 16

Hallie eyed Aiden nervously while he digested the incredible story she'd just told him. They were in his room, the place they'd taken refuge after escaping the maelstrom going on in hers. Jake had been learning a few new tricks, and she'd had no idea he was even capable of the poltergeist behavior she had just witnessed.

Aiden had been forced to duck various objects flying his way until eventually grabbing Hallie's hand and dragging her from the room. After standing outside in the hall for a few minutes, staring at each other in shock and disbelief, they'd made their way silently to Aiden's bedroom.

'Start talking,' Aiden had demanded once the door had closed on them. So she'd told him, all about how Jake had been coming to her since his death and what they'd done to Aiden a few nights earlier. He hadn't spoken again since she'd finished explaining.

Finally, he broke his silence. 'So, he was there the other night?' Hallie nodded. 'Making love to you the same time as I was?'

'He isn't capable of doing everything. He was just kinda touching me. You know, foreplay kind of stuff.'

'Spare me the details, Hallie.'

'Sorry,' she said, as if imploring him to understand. 'I just want to be honest with you.'

'Don't you think the time for honesty was before you dragged me into the middle of some fucked up sex game with your dead husband?' He stopped pacing and laughed then, as if the insanity of what he'd just said hit him. 'He didn't touch me, did he?' The thought had a sobering effect.

'Oh God, no,' she reassured him. 'Jake is as straight as they come, almost to the point of homophobia. In fact, one of the few things we argued about before he died was his attitude towards gay men.'

'Sounds like a charmer.'

'Why are you being so quick to judge him when you just had the exact same reaction to the thought of being touched by a man that he would have done?' Hallie protested, unsure why it mattered to her what Aiden thought of Jake.

'Because I am not gay,' he said calmly, 'and even if I was, I would still be offended that somebody touched me without my consent.'

'Ok.'

'What interests me most,' he said, changing subject, 'is why you thought it was ok to do that to me.'

'I didn't, Aiden. It...it was Jake's idea and I fought him all the way.'

He didn't look convinced. 'So now I am supposed to believe he forced you to do it against your will?'

'It all makes sense if you just let me explain,' she pleaded. 'When he was alive, he had this fantasy of watching me with another man. I never agreed, got mad when he mentioned it in fact.'

'So why now?'

'Because of my attraction to you. Jake and I were, you know, doing stuff one night, and I called out your name.'

She saw his eyes narrow. 'When?'

'The second day, after Cookie got injured.'

'Go on,' he said. Hallie could see a glimmer of male pride in his eyes at the thought he'd had such an effect on her.

'Well, once he knew I'd become attracted to you, he started again with the fantasy stuff, suggesting it could be good for both of us if I brought you up to my room.'

'But you didn't want to?' he asked.

'No. At first, it was just about refusing to give in to Jake. Then, when I got to know you a little better, Jake and his fantasies were the last thing on my mind. I began to want you, so badly, and it made me feel guilty, like I was cheating on my husband.'

'So what happened the night I came to your room? Why did you change your mind?'

Hallie rubbed her eyes tiredly. 'I didn't change my mind. Jake was there when you insisted on coming in. All the while I was looking at you and trying to fight my attraction, Jake was touching me, making me hot, and whispering in my ear about all the things he guessed I wanted you to do to me.' She felt herself blush, the memory too intense. 'So when you came to me, asked me what I wanted, I told you.'

Aiden's face was unreadable. 'What a jerk I am. I thought it was me you were hot for.'

'I was, Aiden. I am.' Hallie took his hands in hers, forcing him to stop pacing as she looked up at him from her place in the chair. 'But I didn't know for sure until last night at the stables. That was just you and I, no games and no Jake, and it felt amazing.' Some of the skepticism left his eyes and it looked as if she could be getting through. 'Come on. You know what happened between us was special. That was the moment I realized that I was beginning to fall for you.'

He pulled his hands away, taking a few steps back as if needing the space to think. 'So treating me like crap all day is your way of showing me how much you care?'

'When I got back to my room last night, I resolved to tell you. Jake didn't want me to, said you wouldn't understand, but I insisted.' Hallie got up to go to him. 'I was terrified at what your reaction would be so I put it off until tonight. That's when I came to your room and found you with Kelly.'

'I explained about Kelly,' he said, brushing the mention of her to one side. 'So what happens now?'

'What do you mean?'

'Us, Hallie. What happens with us?'

She turned away. 'Nothing. You leave in a couple of days, and my life goes back to the way it was.'

'Is that what you want?'

She shook her head. 'No, but it's what has to happen. I can't leave Jake. I'm all he has.'

Aiden's voice rose. 'That's the craziest shit I ever heard. I want you but you push me away so you can stay with a dead husband?'

He'd said he wanted her. The euphoria at his words lasted as long as it took for her to remember it didn't change a thing. 'I want you too but can't you see I have no choice?'

'There is always a choice, Hallie.'

'Not for me. I loved Jake and I still do although not in the same way. How can I desert him?

Aiden fell silent, walking over to stare out of the window into the darkness of the night. 'Has it occurred to you that you may be the reason he is still here? That he can't leave because he knows you need him?'

'No, that's not it,' she said, rejecting an idea that would be too painful to bear if it were true. 'He says he needs me.'

'Yet he'd share you with another man?'

'That's just Jake. Sex is one thing, love is another. He started to get jealous when he realized I was beginning to care for you. I think that's why he tried to stop me telling you about what we'd done.'

Aiden turned to her, the look in his eyes telling her he spoke the truth. 'When I am in love, Hallie, I can't share.' A muscle ticked in his jaw as if just the idea of her with another man made him angry. 'I wouldn't share you.'

'I understand that really I do, which is the reason this has to end.' She walked to the door, preparing to leave. The pain on his face made her feel even worse than she did already. 'I really have no choice. Jake needs me.'

'I need you,' he said, crossing the room to kiss her, crushing her against his chest. Hallie struggled out of his arms, beginning to cry.

'Please don't make this any harder than it is.' She opened the door before he could stop her, stepping through it quickly. 'Goodbye, Aiden.'

Hallie ran to her room, tears streaming down her face as the impact of what she'd just done began to hit her. Had she just thrown away her only chance of real happiness for the love of Jake?

Chapter 17

Hallie dragged herself down to breakfast the next morning, knowing without having to be told by TJ as he met her in the dining room, that Aiden had left. She'd guessed he would, and she didn't blame him for it. She'd have done the same.

'Looks like he checked out late last night. I guess he hitched a ride into town,' TJ said, handing her a sealed envelope and Aiden's room key. 'Left this on the kitchen counter. Maria found it first thing.'

Hallie thrust the envelope into the pocket of her jeans, unwilling to let TJ witness her reaction to what it may contain.

'You ok?' TJ asked, concern furrowing his young brow.

'Just tired I guess.'

'Take the day off. There's not much planned today except for the hayride. Me and Joe can handle that,' he said, mentioning the older man who came in to help out from time to time.

'Thanks,' she smiled, sorely tempted, 'but I'd better show my face. I've played hooky enough this week. Besides, today is the last full day. We can have a break once they leave tomorrow.'

Hallie waited for TJ to wander off before ripping open the envelope. The note inside simply said that he couldn't hang around and watch her throw her life away and that he hoped she'd come to her senses, if only for her own happiness. Aiden had included all this contact details including work and home phone, email and fax. She reread the info he'd provided, wondering why it didn't ring a bell. Surely she'd seen it all before on his booking form?

Having no time to think on it further, she had thrown herself into the chaos of the day, glad for the distraction. Everybody had decided to join in the activities, and Hallie found she had to squeeze herself into a spot on the overloaded wagon between Kelly and Richard. Hallie couldn't think of anyone she wanted to sit next to less but there was just no way to move without making it look personal.

Any hopes Hallie had that Kelly wouldn't bring up the events of the previous night were quickly dashed. 'So, what did you say to Aiden to chase him off?' she asked.

'I'm not sure what you mean,' Hallie said, hoping Kelly wouldn't confess to being in his room when she'd disturbed them, in front of all the other guests.

All eyes turned towards Kelly, and she didn't hesitate in sharing the details with them. 'Last night,' she drawled in explanation. 'Aiden called after we'd all turned in for the night, inviting me to his room.' She turned to Hallie, fixing her without a baleful look. 'But before I could find out what he wanted, as if I didn't know, Hallie showed up.'

'Yeah, sorry about that,' she said, trying to shut down the conversation.

'Thing I don't get,' Kelly continued, 'is that he claimed he never called. I have to confess, I wouldn't have known it was him on the phone unless he'd told me. Some people just sound different I guess.'

'So, did he tell you what he wanted?' Rita asked. Hallie feigned disinterest but kept her ears open, waiting for the answer.

'Like I said, we never got that far. Hallie turned up while he was still denying he'd called. Once she left, he rushed me from the room and went to find her.' Kelly looked at Hallie as if expecting an explanation. Looking around the group, Hallie found them all staring at her with baited breath.

Laughing self consciously, she tried to change the subject. 'We'll soon be arriving at the restaurant I booked for lunch. TJ will give you all vouchers. Just hand them in at the buffet after you've chosen your meals. Drinks aren't included I'm afraid but feel free to use the bar if you want.'

'I wonder who called you,' Rita said, reopening the topic.

'It was him,' Kelly insisted, beginning to get annoyed.

'Why would he deny it?' Ike bellowed, from the far end of the wagon. 'Aiden's a straight shooter. Not like him to play games.'

Kelly started to get flustered. 'Maybe someone was playing tricks on us,' she said accusingly, encompassing the whole group with a suspicious look. They began to protest their innocence so vehemently, Kelly immediately apologized. 'Ok, ok. It was just a thought.'

'Did he give you any idea he planned to leave?' Kelly asked Hallie, determined not to let the mater drop. Hallie shook her head. 'He must have said something.'

'Maybe he left because of you,' Jenny said to Kelly, surprising everyone.

Kelly was taken aback but only temporarily. 'Well, well. Looks like beneath that shy interior beats the heart of a real bitch,' she said, eyes glittering with spite.

'Don't speak to her like that,' Mark said, putting a protective arm around Jenny's shoulder.

'Why not?' said Richard, who Hallie guessed, had just realized he might have a shot at Kelly now Aiden had left. 'Jenny was rude to Kelly.' The Silicon twins glared at each other.

'You have been a little pushy, dear,' Felicity said to Kelly. 'Men don't always respond well to overtly sexual advances.'

'The day I need to take advice from an uptight old maid is the day I hang up my dancing shoes,' Kelly snapped back.

Hey,' bellowed Ike. 'That's enough, little lady.'

Everyone started to talk at once, arguing with some and defending others. Hallie sat in the middle of it all, hands over her ears. The wagon stopped suddenly, and she looked up to find TJ staring at them all as if they were crazy.

Hallie began to laugh, couldn't help it. Tears streamed down her face as the insults continued to fly, each one sending her to a new level of hilarity. Eventually, the others stopped shouting, turning to look at her before beginning to laugh themselves.

Finally, an amicable peace settled over the wagon. TJ got them moving again, after one more deeply bemused look at his passengers. Normal conversation resumed amongst most of the group, and Hallie used the cover of their voices to reassure Kelly that it wasn't her fault Aiden had left. A smile and the small squeeze of her hand she got in reply was Kelly's way of saying thanks.

By the time the wagon pulled up outside the restaurant, they were all friends again.

Chapter 18

'Don't be sad, Hallie,' Jake said, waking her from a wine induced nap later that evening. Hallie jumped to her feet, swearing aloud as she saw the time.

'Oh damn. I am late,' she said, throwing off her clothing as she tore through the room. 'The guests leave tomorrow, and I should be helping Maria get the food ready for the dance tonight.' She pulled the band from hair, tousling the curls and grateful that, for once, it behaved.

'Why are you crying?' Jake persisted, ignoring her.

'Was I?'

'Were you dreaming?'

Hallie stopped struggling with the zipper on her dress. 'I don't think so.' She dropped to her knees, scanning the floor under her bed. 'Where the hell are my shoes?'

'You used to confide in me. Why are you shutting me out?' Jake sounded hurt, but she just didn't have time to deal with him.

'Can we talk about this later? I really have to go help Maria.'

By the time she finished dressing and had slicked a little gloss on her lips and a dab of mascara on her lashes, Jake seemed to have gone. She slipped bright silver hoops into her ears, 'See you later,' she said to the empty room just in case he was still there somewhere.

Reaching the kitchen after a frantic run through the house in perilously high heels, Hallie threw an apron over her black gypsy style dress, apologizing to Maria. 'I am so sorry. What do you need me to do?'

'Relax,' the older woman said, laughing at her flustered state. 'It's all done. TJ is keeping their glasses full, the band is set up in the main hall, and the food is bubbling on the stove.'

'What would I do without you?' Hallie said, sagging in relief as she accepted the glass of wine Maria placed in her hand.

'Work even harder than you do already.' She clucked in disapproval, about to launch into one of her lectures to Hallie about wasting her life hiding away at the ranch.

'I'll just check on the guests,' Hallie said, dashing from the room before Maria could warm to her topic.

'Don't forget to take off that apron,' she heard Maria say before the door closed.

Her entrance into the main room was greeted with a small cheer from the guests; already well on their way to intoxication thanks to TJ's diligent efforts. The four piece country band already playing lifted everyone's spirits even higher with a raucous version of a Garth Brooks favorite. Some of the younger guests were already on the floor, throwing themselves around wildly. Hallie smiled, genuinely pleased to see them having so much fun.

She got a lump in her throat as she remembered that one man was conspicuous by his absence. Hallie got the feeling he would have enjoyed seeing how many friendships had been forged in the brief time the group had spent together.

'Hey there, little lady,' Ike said, dragging her from thoughts of Aiden. 'It's about time we had that dance.'

'Are you sure Felicity won't mind?' she teased as she took his hand.

'Hell, no,' he bellowed into her ear, making her wince. 'It was her idea. She said you looked like you needed cheering up.'

'I'm fine. This has been a wonderful week, and you are all wonderful people.' Hallie swallowed back tears she knew had nothing to do with the guests present at the party. 'So Ike,' she said, changing the subject. 'What's the story with you and Felicity?'

The big man blushed uncharacteristically. 'She's a great lady,' he said quietly, casting a look her way. 'I hope she stays in touch.'

'I'm sure she will.' Hallie gave Ike a squeeze before stepping out of his arms as she noticed Maria and TJ beginning to bring in the food.

The meal went well. Maria had outdone herself as usual, and the guests all congratulated her on the wonderful banquet she had prepared. Hallie and the rest of the staff of the Sleepy Hills Ranch were surprised and delighted to find out that the guests had purchased gifts for them.

Hallie gasped when she tore open her package to reveal an antique lace shawl. 'We got it in town,' Kelly explained, eyes shining with tears that mirrored Hallie's. 'We hope you like it.'

'It's beautiful. Thank you all so much,' she managed to say before her voice broke on a sob. Maria didn't fare much better when she saw that her gift was a huge, framed picture of herself, working in the kitchen. The photographer had caught her essence—head thrown back on a full bodied laugh, eyes twinkling with kindness and mirth, hands buried in bread dough. A view of the mountains through the kitchen window provided the back drop to the picture, shrouding Maria in the warm, soft light cast over the ranch at dawn.

Hallie could guess who the photographer had been. Sharon, the nurse who had seemed so boisterous and outgoing at first, had settled quietly into the group once she'd realized there was little chance of romance for her this time out. The expensive looking camera she had taken everywhere probably contained some wonderful photos and memories. Hallie reminded herself to ask her to send copies once she got home. It would be interesting to see some shots of the ranch. Maybe Aiden would be in some of them.

TJ was in turn very pleased with his t-shirt. 'Head Honcho at The Sleepy Hills Ranch' was emblazoned across the back of the garment while his initials were embroidered over the chest pocket. Everyone laughed as TJ stripped off the t-shirt he wore to put on his new one, seeming not to care that he was undressing at the dining table. Maria clucked in her usual fashion as she saw his skinny frame, saying aloud for the umpteenth time that she needed to 'fatten that boy up.'

'I think he's lovely,' said Kelly, giving him a saucy wink that made his cheeks go almost the exact same shade as his red hair. Hallie wished Kelly wouldn't tease him so much. The twenty-year-old had the biggest crush on her and, when he hadn't been following Aiden around in near adoration. Hallie knew she could always find him wherever Kelly was.

Everyone helped with the clean up, including the band who had retired to the kitchen to eat their supper at the work table. It wasn't long before the party was in full swing again. The band, comprised of a fiddle, a banjo, a guitar and a double bass, started a square dance to get everyone up on their feet, calling out the instructions to the great hilarity of the guests.

'Don't worry,' giggled Hallie, as Mark and Richard careened their dance partners into each other, 'it's funnier when you get it wrong.' Everyone fell about laughing as they realized that Ike and Felicity had collided with Milton and Rita, and in the resulting confusion, had managed to end up with the wrong partners.

Hallie paired up with TJ and began to wonder how much wine he had managed to sneak this time. She always had to keep an eye on him at parties, often finding him giggly and tipsy in a corner. He always denied he'd touched a drop but then, like this time, the glazed eyes and a dopey grin gave him away.

TJ began to spin her faster, whooping and hollering as they spun. Suddenly, he let her go, making Hallie twist on her heel and afraid she would fall, until her body hit something solid and warm, stopping her dead in her tracks. Strong arms closed around her as Hallie struggled to get a proper look at the face she'd seen briefly just before she collided with its owner.

Aiden smiled at her shocked expression. 'If you wanted to dance, darlin', you only had to ask.'

Chapter 19

'What are you doing here?' she asked, trying to pull her hand from his as he dragged her from the room and out of the view of prying and interested eyes.

'Aren't you pleased to see me?' he asked, allowing his gaze to drift down to the shoulder exposed by the neckline of her dress slipping as she had struggled, 'because I am sure pleased to see you.'

'Really?' she said carefully, unwilling to let him know just how totally thrilled she was to see him again. 'Is that why you left without saying goodbye?'

The smile left his face. 'I had a lot to think about. Be fair, Hallie. How would you have reacted?'

He was right but that wasn't the point, she thought angrily. 'Be grateful that you have the choice. I can't just run away from the situation.'

'I know. And I'm sorry. I handled it all wrong.' His smile began to warm her insides and she felt herself being drawn nearer. Hallie brushed his hand away as he tried to caress her bare shoulder. She needed to keep a clear head.

'So you came back to apologize? Okay, I accept your apology.' She couldn't afford to let him get close and folded her arms across her chest, trying to force him to keep his distance with an icy tone. 'Can I get back to my guests now?'

Aiden blushed. 'We need to talk. I haven't been entirely truthful.'

'What do you mean?'

'I didn't come to the ranch for a holiday or to find love,' he said. 'Truth is I bought the neighboring ranch a few months back.'

She was shocked. 'Sleepy Creek? That place has been derelict for years.'

He nodded. 'I had plans to set it up, offer a similar operation to yours but much larger. I planned some radical expansion. You know, take it to the next level.'

Hallie understood. 'So you came here to check out the competition?'

Aiden began to squirm. 'It's a little more than that. My plan was to buy you out too and use your land. I just needed to see for myself how you were doing and what I was up against.'

'And it didn't occur to you to introduce yourself and ask if I wanted to sell up?'

'I didn't know you then, or how I was going to feel about you.' His eyes begged her to believe him, the hope dimming as she took another step back. 'It's the way I have always done business. Scout out the competition, find their weaknesses and strengths, and play to them.'

'So you heard about the poor widow struggling to keep her ranch going on her own and thought it would be easy to exploit her. Was that it?' Hallie couldn't believe what he was saying.

Aiden looked offended. 'No. I'd have given you a fair price. Do you think so little of me?'

'No, I guess not,' she said, anger slipping away. He wasn't the first person who had expressed an interest in the ranch, and she could hardly be offended at the actions of a man who had not known her until a week ago. 'You could have been honest though.'

'That's the reason I came back,' he said, encouraged by the calmness of her reaction. 'I got all bent out of shape when you told me about Jake, and I put a huge guilt trip on you about it. I was on the road back to Phoenix before it hit to me that I hadn't been entirely truthful either.'

'Maybe you came back to take another stab at getting me to sell up to you,' she said, not believing that was his intention but needing to hear him say it.

'Hell, I knew you wouldn't sell this place the day Cookie got hurt. I saw your face just before the accident. You love this land, and I can tell it holds a lot of memories for you.' Hallie nodded, unable to trust her voice as a lump rose in her throat. 'Buying the ranch may have been the reason I came, but it isn't why I stayed.'

She didn't fight when he began to pull her close again. Hallie sighed as she relaxed into his arms, allowing herself a brief moment of comfort before she pushed him away, as she knew she must. Aiden kissed her, and Hallie groaned with the urge to take him upstairs to her room and claim him again. She wanted him and it seemed so unfair all of a sudden that she was trapped in a relationship that met none of her needs.

'Aiden, stop,' she said, pulling away. 'There's no point to this. I haven't changed my mind about Jake.'

'But I have,' he said, shocking her for the second time. 'If the only way I can have you is to share you with Jake, then I guess I can learn to live with it.'

'Are you serious?'

'Yes. I'd be lying if I said I didn't want you all to myself but that isn't an option right now.' Aiden frowned as a thought hit him. 'That's if you still want me.'

'I do,' Hallie said, confused by the turn of events, 'but not like this. It isn't fair to any of us.'

'Look, I thought about what you said. If I loved someone as much as you loved Jake, I couldn't desert them either. Even if I succeeded in taking you away from here, you could never be happy knowing that he was here alone and waiting for you. But I am not prepared to be without you. So this is the only option.'

She didn't know what to say. Hallie didn't even know if what he'd just said made her happy or sad. And how would Jake feel?

Somehow, Hallie didn't think he'd react well to the news that Aiden was planning to stick around. 'I need time to think.'

'To hell with thinking.' Aiden was getting angry. 'If Jake's death proved anything to you it should be that life is too short to be away from the people you love.'

Love? Aiden loved her too? Hallie's heart leapt and then sunk instantly as she realized that it didn't matter that he felt the same way she did. Jake didn't mind sharing her body but he wouldn't share her heart.

'It's just not that simple,' Hallie said, tears streaming down her face as she ran blindly up the stairs to her bedroom.

Chapter 20

'You don't get rid of me so easily this time,' Aiden said, walking into her room without knocking. Hallie jumped from the bed where she had thrown herself moments earlier to cry out her disappointment, hurt and rage at the unfairness of the situation. Jake had tried to console her but she'd told him to leave her alone. Hallie knew he was still in the room somewhere. She wondered what he would make of Aiden turning up.

'I'm not trying to get rid of you. Don't you see, there is just no way this can work.'

'Didn't you tell him about me?' asked Jake, from his place in the corner.

'Yes, Jake, I told you I did.'

'He's here now?' Aiden looked around as if trying to find him. Hallie nodded.

'What does he want?' Jake said.

'I don't know, why don't you ask him?' Hallie snapped.

'Who are you talking to, me or him?' asked Aiden.

'Oh God, this is making me crazy,' she said, turning her back on the pair of them.

'Why?' Aiden and Jake asked at the same time. Hallie almost laughed. How crazy was this?

'Because, both of you are pulling at me, and I can't think straight.'

Hallie heard the door close and spun around, expecting to discover that Aiden had left. Instead, she found him unbuckling his jeans. 'What are you doing?' she asked stupidly as he pulled his shirt free and began to unbutton it. Aiden shrugged off the rest of his clothes, kicking his boots across the room with abandon.

'He's going to fuck you,' Jake said with a slight laugh, as if he admired the other man's audacity. 'Now there's a guy who knows what he wants.'

The breath caught in her throat. She was torn between feeling totally cornered and unbearably hot at the thought of what may be about to happen. If she admitted the truth, the night they had both taken her would have been one of the best experiences of her life if she hadn't had to deal with the guilt of knowing that she was deceiving one of them. This time, if it happened, everyone would be willing.

'You know you want this, Hallie,' Jake urged, voice getting heavy. 'I sure as hell do.'

Dare she take what was being offered by two men who loved and wanted her and claimed they didn't mind sharing?

'I'm not giving up,' Aiden said, walking towards her purposefully, his penis already beginning to harden. She was sure he could see the excitement and trepidation in her and it was spurring him on. 'You look amazing in that dress by the way.' He reached for her, dragging the elasticized neckline down as far as he could, exposing her shoulders and the swell of her breasts.

'Jake is still here,' she said hoarsely.

'I know.'

'Don't you mind?'

Aiden didn't answer immediately, his attention focused solely on licking every inch of skin he had exposed. 'Uh uh.'

'I don't know if I can do this,' she protested weakly, pulling Aiden's head closer to the nipples he was sucking at through the fabric.

'Is Jake going to join us?' he asked, sliding his hands down her thighs to drag the skirt up her legs.

'I'm already here,' Jake whispered in her ear, brushing invisible fingers over the skin exposed by Aiden. 'It makes me so fucking hot that you would do this for me.'

'Jake, I'm not doing this for you. This is for me,' she said, reaching down to sheath Aiden's cock with her palms.

'It's all for you, baby,' Aiden said, reaching around her to unzip the dress, allowing it to fall to her feet. Forcing Hallie to sit on the bed after removing her panties, he was about to kneel between her knees.

'Suck his cock,' Jake said, voice hoarse, his touch on her nipples getting harder and more persistent. 'Let me see your lips around him.'

She dragged Aiden down beside her on the bed, forcing him to lie back as she took his prick in her hands, flicking a tongue over the tip once or twice before opening her mouth and allowing him in slowly. He groaned as her lips began to slide over his skin, and she felt the muscles in his thighs begin to tremble with the urge to thrust into her.

'I bet that feels fucking amazing,' Jake said, continuing to caress her breasts as she leaned over Aiden, kissing her neck. 'You were always so good at giving head.'

'Is he watching?' Aiden asked. Hallie nodded, almost smiling as Aiden clasped her head as his cock surged at her answer. Looked like her husband wasn't the only one with a little kinkiness in his soul. Jake's mouth began to kiss and lick its way down her back, lingering on her buttocks, keeping her waiting a moment longer before she felt his touch on her clit.

Hallie groaned, throat opening wide to allow more of Aiden into her mouth as Jake's touch made her tremble. She could feel his hands on her thighs and pictured him lying between her legs, tongue working feverishly over her flesh.

'What is he doing?' Aiden asked, becoming aware of her arousal.

'He's sucking my clit,' she said breathlessly as she lifted her head, stroking Aiden's cock with her hand. The expression on his face confused her for a moment. If she didn't know better, she'd think he was angry at what she'd just said. Hallie forgot about any of that as

Aiden reached for her, dragging her body over his and forcing her to sit on his face.

He did what Jake never could. His fingers parted her labia, allowing his tongue to swirl over every part of her swollen flesh. He sucked her into his mouth, sliding a thick finger inside her and beginning to slowly but firmly fuck her.

'Hey, no fair,' Jake protested, moving behind her. 'I can't get to you.'

Hallie wanted to ignore his voice and focus on the orgasm she could feel Aiden's mouth pulling from her but she couldn't. Jake was here too, and it seemed only fair that she did as much as she could to include him. She tried to get up but Aiden grabbed her thighs in his hands, forcing her back down onto him.

'I…I need to move,' she said, voice beginning to weaken as Aiden's head moved faster, taking her over the brink, her body shuddering as the waves of pleasure hit her out of the blue. He didn't let her go until her the last spasms had trickled through her.

'He did that on purpose,' Jake said, sounding angry. 'He's trying to shut me out.'

'I don't think so.' Hallie gave Aiden a questioning look as she repeated what Jake had just said.

Aiden shrugged, faking nonchalance but his eyes blazed in triumph. 'Sorry.'

'What do you want us to do, Jake?' she asked pointedly, giving Aiden a warning look. She should have known not to trust him.

'Sit on his cock and ride him hard,' Jake said, anger forgotten. 'I want to be able to touch you too.'

Hallie did as she was told but began to think that having two men in bed with her should mean twice the pleasure not twice the work. She crawled across Aiden's body and aligned her groin over his. He took over, holding himself upright and guiding her pussy down onto his dick with a strong hand.

Her eyes closed as Aiden's cock filled her to the brink. He began to writhe beneath her, pushing up harder and faster as his breathing got more and more ragged. She felt Jake's mouth on her breasts as his fingers played over her clitoris and anus at the same time.

Aiden seemed frustrated by his position below her and slammed into her hard, as if unable to get deep enough. Jake, on the other hand, seemed happy where he was and determined to make her come, as if using Aiden's cock as a vibrator. 'Can you feel me?' he kept asking, over and over. Hallie groaned her answer, reassuring Jake that she could although she found it hard to concentrate on anything else but Aiden's penis buried deep inside her.

Jake increased the pressure, rubbing her clit hard as she heard his breath begin to falter. Relief flooded through her at the sound of his orgasm. Her own body began to respond once she no longer had to worry about him. She came moments later, quivering helplessly as the two men each did their best to ensure that they alone were the reason for her climax.

'Ok, I'm done sharing,' Aiden said, throwing her off him to roll on top of her, almost hiding her from view with his massive frame. He parted her legs, entering her wet, warm pussy with one huge thrust. He clasped her head in his hands, searing her lips with a kiss as he began to ride her hard.

Hallie couldn't think as he totally dominated all of her senses. Jake probably wasn't happy about it but he seemed to have given up.

'Open your eyes,' Aiden said, barely able to speak as his orgasm began. 'I want you to know it's me.' His voice cracked as his body began to jerk as the first violent waves hit him. 'Say my name, Hallie.'

She gave him what he wanted, staring into his eyes and speaking his name over and over as he thrashed above her. Aiden struggled to hold her gaze until the last, as if determined to savor every moment. As the final spasms subsided, he sank on top of her, kissing her gently before rolling away and drawing her to him.

'He had no intention of sharing you, Hallie,' she heard Jake say from across the room a few minutes later. 'He came here tonight to claim you.'

Unable to answer him, Hallie had no choice but to allow his words to echo around her head. Jake was right but she couldn't judge Aiden for it. Part of her thrilled to the knowledge of just how far he would go to have her but it wasn't fair to any of them to let the situation continue.

'I don't want you to see him anymore.'

'We can talk about this later, Jake,' Hallie whispered, glad that Aiden had been exhausted enough to fall asleep as soon as his head hit the pillow, totally unfazed by Jake's presence it seemed.

'Make him leave.' She shook her head. 'Either he goes or I do,' Jake threatened.

'I am not going to kick him out of bed just because you say so.'

Jake went silent but Hallie knew he was still in the room. Her suspicions were confirmed as the curtains at the window began to billow and the framed picture on the mantel began to slide towards the edge. This time, it didn't crash to the floor but instead seemed to float through the air, coming closer to the bed before hovering over Aiden's head.

'Jake, if you hit him with that I will never forgive you,' she whispered urgently, dropping her voice even lower as Aiden stirred. 'I'll leave you, Jake. That's a promise.' The picture stayed where it was.

'Okay, okay,' Jake said as the picture dropped gently onto Hallie's lap. 'There's no need to pitch a fit.'

Jake left without saying another word, and Hallie sighed, wondering what the hell she should do. Picking up the frame that held a picture of the happiest day of her life, her eyes drifted lovingly over Jake's face, and she smiled as she remembered the feelings that had caused the adoring look she was giving her new husband.

She placed the picture on the nightstand before turning away from it to stare at Aiden's sleeping form. Her heart raced as she studied him in detail. He'd told her that life was too short to be away from the people he loved and she knew she loved him right back, in a way she had never thought she would again. Hallie knew there could never be a repeat of what happened in her room tonight. Neither Jake nor Aiden had it in them to truly share. Both of them were Alpha male to the bone and had far more in common than they realized.

Hallie looked at the beautiful man in bed beside her and knew he could be her future, but only if she could walk away from her past.

Chapter 21

Hallie mounted Dylan, Cookie's stable mate, and rode him quietly from the yard. Dawn had barely broken, and she hadn't slept a wink all night.

The pink light of sunrise tinted the mountain tops, and the air was still crisp and fresh. She shuddered in the thin t-shirt and jacket, wishing she'd been able to get a sweater out of the drawer but she hadn't wanted to risk waking Aiden. They needed to talk but first she wanted time to think without the distraction of his all-seeing green eyes and distracting body. He'd turned over in bed just before she sneaked from the room, and the sheet had slipped to rest in the crook of his hip. He'd thrown an arm across his face in his sleep to shield his eyes from the early morning light, stretching out his long torso. Hallie thought he looked like an Elgin marble, perfect in shape and form.

Aiden. Just thinking about him made her heart race. That was until she remembered Jake. The man she had married. The man who had broken her heart by dying.

What had seemed like a rare blessing at first—discovering that he was still with her despite his death—had become a curse. Hallie felt a pang of guilt as she always did when she allowed herself to think of where she would be now if Jake had simply died. Would she have kept the ranch or still met Aiden?

She didn't yet know how she would do it, but she had to find a way to convince Jake it was time to go. With or without Aiden's influence, Hallie knew she had to move on.

An hour into her ride, she realized she should have checked on the weather before setting out. Dark, ominous cloud began to blot out the sky, and she heard a distant rumble of thunder. Dylan began to get skittish as she turned him around to head for home.

She'd taken a little known trail, one that Jake and she had ridden many times when they wanted to get away from other people. Even TJ didn't know about it. The track was a narrow one, snaking its way through the trees, rising slowly towards the foot of the mountain. Hallie kicked Dylan into a trot, aware that the storm was getting nearer. It hadn't yet begun to rain, and she hoped it would hold off until she got onto level ground.

Suddenly, a bolt of lightning split the sky, hitting a tree off to her right. The strike hadn't been that close but it spooked the usually calm horse. Dylan reared up on his hind legs, sending Hallie flying towards the ground as he lost his footing. She landed on her side, curling into a ball and putting her hands over her head instinctively, aware that the horse was beginning to stumble. Stones and twigs billowed around her as Dylan's feet tried to get purchase. Hallie felt his hoof on her shin and cried out in pain as she heard the bone snap.

A wave of nausea surged through her as she kept her eyes on Dylan, bracing herself, ready to roll out of the way should he fall. Finally, he found his legs and kicked more dirt in her face as he bolted away, still shaken by the lightning strike. Hallie whistled as loudly as she could, praying the horse would stop close by. If she could just get herself into the saddle, she could ride them both out of the storm and home to safety. But Dylan kept on running.

Hallie looked around for something to use to help her get to her feet. A cluster of boulders a few feet down the hill seemed her best chance, and she grimaced in agony as she dragged herself towards them.

Her progress had been slow and tiring, and Hallie needed a few minutes to catch her breath before she tried to get up. She bit her lip in anticipation of the pain as she used her good leg and a grip on the rock to get her onto her feet. Her other leg screamed in protest and she began to cry softly, putting off the moment she would have to test her weight on it, knowing it would be unbearable. Nothing prepared her for the searing pain that shot through her as she tried to straighten out her knee. Hallie thought she was going to throw up and began to shake as she braced herself against the rock and slid back down onto her butt.

What the fuck was she going to do? She whistled for Dylan, craning her neck to see if she could spot him through the trees but he appeared to have gone. Maybe he'd head back to the ranch, alerting someone to her absence. But what good would it do, she berated herself. Nobody but Jake knew about this place.

The rain began, coming down hard and compounding her misery. Hallie shrugged off her jacket, using it to shield her head from the downpour. She crouched further into the rock, trying to drag her legs out of the way of the small river beginning to trickle down the dirt track, caused by the deluge. Shivers wracked her body as her clothing was drenched by the violent storm. The cold seeped into her bones, making her broken leg slightly less painful as it began to get numb. She fought to keep her eyes open to look for her horse but the desire to close them was overwhelming, and she couldn't see much through the heavy curtain of water anyway.

Hallie's head began to fall forward as she gave in to the sudden exhaustion seeping into her body.

Chapter 22

Hallie's head jerk up painfully, the stiffness in her frozen neck catching her by surprise. Unsure what had woken her, she looked around in confusion. The thunder looked to be moving away, taking the worst of the rain with it. Thin drizzle continued to fall but she could see much clearer than before. Still no sign of Dylan. She'd hoped for a brief moment that the horse had returned.

'Hallie?'

'Yes,' she screamed, turning in the direction of the voice.

'It's me.'

'Jake,' she sighed, sagging back against the rock. Great, now she was hallucinating.

'Hallie, are you okay? What happened?'

What if it really was Jake? Maybe he'd found a way to speak to her. 'What are you doing here?' A thought hit her. 'Am I dead?'

'No, you're not dead. Where are you?' he asked, confusing her.

'At the pass, near the boulders at the foot of the mountain. Where are you?'

'I am still at the ranch. And before you ask, I don't know why I am able to talk to you out here. I guess I just never tried before. What happened? When Dylan came back without a rider, TJ came up to check on you. Aiden answered the door to him.'

'Has anyone but you figured out where I am?' she asked hopefully.

'Not yet, Hallie, but I am trying to figure out a way to let them know.'

'Okay.' Hallie fell silent, desolate that the one person who knew where she was couldn't help her at all.

'Fuck, I feel so damn useless,' Jake said angrily before turning his frustration on her. 'What in the hell were you doing out here before the sun was up?'

'I needed time to think.'

'About what?'

Hallie tried to smile. 'Take a wild guess.'

'Aiden?'

'Not just Aiden. You too.'

She heard him sigh. 'You shouldn't waste your time thinking about me. It's my fault that you are even in this mess.'

'It's nobody's fault. Who knew how things were going to turn out?'

'I tried to force you to stay with me. It wasn't fair on you.'

'I wouldn't have had it any other way,' she reassured him, waiting a moment before continuing, 'but it's time for both of us to move on.'

'I know.'

His reply surprised her. For the first time, they were actually talking about letting go, no ifs, buts or maybes. The thought scared her.

'How the hell am I going to let that giant blond idiot know where you are?' Jake said, laughing to soften his words. 'He's out looking for you now.'

'Poor Aiden,' she said, before remembering the insult. 'Hey, don't call him that.'

'I'm kidding, Hallie. He seems like a good man. I can trust him to take care of you.' He chuckled. 'Can't say I'm too happy that he muscled in on me last night, but I guess I like the fact he seemed prepared to fight for you.'

'He can be hard to ignore.'

'Maybe it's for the best. He knew what I was doing to you was wrong. Without him, who knows how long this would have gone on?'

Hallie felt the tears swell in her chest as pain mingled with sadness at the growing knowledge this could be the last time she would ever speak to Jake. 'Having you here kept me going. I love you even more for coming back to take care of me and getting me through those awful first months after you died. Don't ever be sorry for what we shared. I'm not,' she said fiercely.

'My feisty little girl,' he said affectionately, taking her back to the day they'd first met in high school. He'd called her that ever since he'd found her taking on a group of older boys who'd been bullying a kid. 'There's one other thing I better tell you too.'

'What?' Hallie's eyes were beginning to droop again.

'Kelly. Aiden didn't call her. I got one of my friends to do it.'

'It doesn't matter now,' she said sleepily. 'You have friends?'

Jake sounded sheepish. 'That's something else I didn't tell you. I figured you wouldn't want to stay with me if you knew that things over here are not so bad. I didn't mean to trick you. I just wasn't ready to let you go.'

'It's ok, I understand.'

Hallie began to drift in and out of consciousness. She woke up briefly in panic, thinking he had gone. 'Don't leave me yet. I don't want to be alone.'

'I'm always gonna be right here, baby, even if you don't know it.' His voice was soothing, and she closed her eyes again, knowing that he would watch over her after he had gone. 'I will never stop loving you, Hallie.'

'I love you too Jake.'

A tear slid gently down her cheek as calmness descended over her as her husband's soul set her free.

* * * *

She dreamed of Jake during long hours spent sleeping fitfully on the side of the mountain. As the morning stretched into the afternoon and on into the night, her dreams were of their life together before Aiden. Hallie saw herself again at his funeral and cried bitter tears as she truly said goodbye.

She dreamed of Aiden too, seeing him searching for her. Hallie could almost hear him calling her name but she knew it was only her imagination. Nobody but a dead man and a horse knew where she lay.

'Wake up,' Jake whispered in her ear. Her eyes fluttered open in confusion. Was she still asleep?

She heard Aiden call her name again, sure this time that she wasn't dreaming. 'I'm here,' she shouted as loud as she could, despite the dehydration and exhaustion draining her voice. 'Aiden, I'm here,' she said, over and over, fighting the tiredness dragging her under. Maybe she'd only imagined she heard him. Hallie passed out again until a scuffling on the hill beside her jerked her awake. She squinted against a bright light in her eyes, gasping in fear until the flashlight dipped and she saw Aiden's face.

She began to cry, burying her face into the warmth and strength of his chest as he dropped to his knees and crushed her to him. 'Thank God,' Aiden said repeatedly as he ran his hands over her body, checking for more damage. 'I've been looking for you all day, getting more and more terrified as the hours wore on.'

'How did you find me,' she said, her voice muffled by his chest. Hallie had Aiden in her arms and didn't intend to let go of him any time soon.

'Jake.' Aiden shook his head. 'At least, I think it was Jake.'

'How?'

'Damned if I know. I was riding out at the creek about two hours ago and then suddenly, Dylan just began to ignore me, taking off like he was chasing a mare through the fields. He led me up the path to this place, and thank God he did. I'd never have found you otherwise.'

'Jake was with me here the whole time. He came to watch over me and to say goodbye.' Hallie could see Aiden understood the sadness in her voice, and he didn't question her further.

'Ok, Hallie, you are gonna have to be brave for me so I can move you. This terrain is too rough for a vehicle, and we need to get you to a hospital. We've got no choice but to ride out of here.' She nodded, understanding the reason but wanting to cry at the thought of the pain she would have to endure. 'Ready?' He lifted her into his arms and onto Dylan's back in one move.

Hallie felt the saddle beneath her butt and let out the breath she'd been holding to stop her screaming out. Scaring the horse again would do nobody any good, and she wept at the effort her silence had cost her as she slumped against the animal's neck.

Aiden climbed up behind her, putting his jacket over her shoulders before wrapping a strong arm around her body and pulling her back against his chest. As he urged Dylan gently forwards the motion sent a wave of nausea and pain through Hallie, and she felt herself slip into semi-consciousness once more as Aiden whispered in her ear that she was safe.

The next few hours passed by in a blur. Vague memories of car journeys, bright lights and doctors were all she would remember of the rest of that day, but the comforting touch of Aiden's hand, gripping hers tightly, stayed with her always.

Chapter 23

'So, what do you think of the place?' Aiden asked nervously as Hallie walked slowly through each room of the rundown ranch.

'I don't know. There's a lot of work to be done. It needs rebuilding from the ground up,' she said, leaning her crutches against the wall. 'Do you have the time and money for this kind of project?'

'Money is not a problem,' he said, confirming her suspicions that he was pretty wealthy. He'd been able to walk away from his life in Phoenix without a backward glance. Aiden took her arm, allowing her to lean on him as she hobbled around on the cast encasing her lower leg. 'Should you be walking around so much?'

'It's fine.' She smiled. 'I've been going crazy confined to the house for the last three weeks. I can't tell you how good it is to get out of there.'

Aiden chuckled, tipping his hat. 'Glad to be of service, ma'am.'

Hallie rolled her eyes at his over-the-top charm. Secretly, she found it cute but she could never resist the urge to tease him. 'Steady on, cowboy.'

They reached the bottom of a long staircase. Aiden picked her up without a word and took the steps two at a time, barely breaking a sweat as they reached the top. He didn't put her down as he strode the length of the corridor towards a room at the far end of the hall.

'Get the door for me,' he said, dipping her so she could reach the handles. The huge mahogany panels swung wide, opening into an enormous space. 'I've chosen this one as the master bedroom.'

Hallie gave a low whistle as she took in the massive iron bed nestled between two floor length windows on the main wall.

Everything had recently been given a fresh coat of magnolia paint, making the room look bright and clean. Gauzy curtains blocked out the harsh sunlight, casting a warm glow over the Mexican style furniture. Even the bed had been made and covered in a pretty red and cream embroidered throw that she recognized as Maria's handiwork.

'So this is what you've been up to.' Hallie had wondered where he'd kept disappearing to for hours on end. After keeping his room at Sleepy Hills and paying in full despite Hallie's objections, he'd spent barely any time in it or with her. In fact, Hallie's frustration was beginning to reach boiling point. Aiden hadn't laid a hand on her since the accident, afraid that he would hurt her. She wasn't so sure that had been the real reason but Aiden would say no more, going back to his room alone every night, despite her best attempts to turn him on. She smiled secretly as she remembered how aroused he had become. Still, he hadn't succumbed.

'This is for us, Hallie,' he said as he placed her gently on top of the bed. 'I wanted us to have a place of our own.'

'It's beautiful, but you didn't need to do this.'

His face became serious. 'Yes, I did. I know Jake has gone but it just felt kinda wrong to start our life together in his house.'

'It's my house too,' she reminded him gently, encouraging him to sit beside her.

'I know but that's not the point. I feel like Jake trusted me, you know? It just seemed disrespectful to try and forget he was ever there.' Aiden sighed as if unsure he'd made his point. 'That bed belonged to you and Jake and you'd still be in it together if it wasn't for some freak accident that robbed you both. I've got no desire to trample all over his memory by trying to take his place.'

Hallie felt deeply touched by his respect for her dead husband but she suspected there was more to the story that he wasn't saying. 'I love you even more for that, Aiden,' she said, kissing his lips. 'I must confess, I have been wondering myself if he has really gone or just decided not to get in our way anymore.'

Aiden smiled, relief flooding his handsome features. 'You too? I thought I was the only one thinking that way.' He brushed a strand of her from her neck, placing his lips on the exposed skin and trailing his tongue over it. 'Besides, I don't want to have to think of him watching me do what I want to do.'

'What do you want to do?' Hallie urged, praying this wasn't going to be another frustrating experiment in foreplay like the kind she'd had to endure since she got hurt. Aiden had a gifted mouth and talented hands and had left her almost begging to be fucked every time he'd touched her over the last few weeks. 'Don't start anything you don't intend to finish,' she warned him, smiling as his hand slipped under her dress.

'Oh, I won't,' he promised, scratching his nails across the inside of her thigh. Hallie parted her legs for him as his mouth continued its path across her collarbone and down over her cleavage. Lifting her butt from the bed, she allowed him to pull her panties off before throwing them away carelessly.

Aiden dropped to his knees, burying his head between her thighs and lapping at her hot flesh. Hallie began to quiver as her insides coiled around the finger he slid into her pussy. She began to wiggle against his hand, trying to increase the friction and bring on the orgasm he had denied her for too long.

'Please Aiden,' she begged as he lifted his head to watch her reaction to the movements of his hand. Putting her legs gently over his shoulder, he continued to fuck her with a strong finger as he sucked her clit into his hot mouth. Hallie exploded almost immediately, shaking and crying as wave after wave of spasms rippled through her pussy.

Hallie stood shakily as soon as he released her, shrugging off her dress and remaining underwear. Using her good leg, she pushed back across the bed and waited for him to join her. 'If you think that's all its gonna take to satisfy me, then you are sadly mistaken,' she purred.

Amused by the look on his face, she allowed her legs to fall open and she stroked her still sensitive flesh.

Aiden ripped off his clothing, eyes fixed on her hand as he crawled towards her. Grabbing the back of her thighs, he dragged her ass further down the bed, hooking her knees over his arms to spread her wide in readiness. His golden head dropped to watch as he pushed his hard cock into her still moist pussy, shoulders quivering with the effort it took not to let his weight fall on her.

'Fuck, that feels good,' he groaned, reaching up for a kiss, sliding his tongue into her mouth. Hallie sucked on it, simulating the way her body clasped at his prick.

The bed began to rock as he used her hips to pull her onto him repeatedly. Hallie's broken leg rested safely over his forearm as she moved her other to brace it against the mattress, allowing her to push back against him, answering his thrusts with her own.

Hallie laced her hands through his hair, turning his head to bite into his shoulder, holding the flesh between her teeth as their bodies rocked back and forth.

'Ah, that's it, baby,' he said, encouraging her to increase the pressure.

Reaching as far down as she could, she sank her nails into his back and dragged them over his skin. Aiden hissed and threw his head back, pummeling her harder. Hallie's hips left the bed, and she pushed back onto his cock as hard as she could.

His brow creased as a grimace masked his handsome face when he began to come. His head dropped to her shoulder as he jerked above her, gasping loudly with each thrust, fingers digging into her hip as the last of the spasms rocked his long, tanned body.

Aiden eased away from her shakily, collapsing beside her as soon as he was clear of her injured leg. Hallie turned towards him with care, moving the cast to one side so she could hook her good leg over his shin and prop her head up on her palm to look at him.

'Welcome home,' he said with a crooked grin that didn't mask the emotion in his eyes. She realized just how much it all meant to him. Intending to drop a quick kiss on his lips, Hallie found her head trapped by a large hand as it deepened into something with much more meaning.

'I love this place,' she said, tears beginning to form as she saw the delighted smile he gave in response.

He sat up, enthusiasm making him talk in a rush as he explained his plans for the house in full. Aiden didn't mention Sleepy Hills although she knew her decision over what to do with the ranch was central to their future.

She would tell him later that she wanted the same as him eventually, to start a new life in a home they could call their own. Her place could play an important part in the development of what would be the largest dude ranch in the county. But it was early days, both in their relationship and in the redevelopment of the house and its surrounding land. By the time everything was ready, she would be too.

'So, what do you think?' he asked, heart in his eyes. 'Could you be happy here, with me?'

'I'll tell you in a minute,' she said, teasing him as she slid slowly from the bed and hobbled over to a window. She smiled as her eyes took in the view. Her beloved mountain seemed to rise up to greet her, its jagged peak silhouetted in the darkening sky.

Aiden joined her, wrapping his naked body around hers as he stared at the view. 'That mountain is the reason I chose this room for you,' he said. 'As long as you can see it, you know you are home.'

Hallie turned in his arms, accepting his kiss as he told her he loved her. 'I love you too, Aiden.'

The chill began to bite at her skin until Aiden carried her back to the bed, folding his body around hers as they prepared to spend their first night together in the house that represented their future.

She fell asleep in his arms, to dreams of Jake, smiling down on her from his place on the mountain. 'Be free, Hallie, and live for both of us,' he said, blowing her a kiss before fading away.

Hallie smiled in her sleep, promising that she would relish every moment and grab at her chance of true happiness again with Aiden— for the love of Jake.

THE END

WWW.LUXIERYDER.COM

[Siren Menage Amour 25: Menage a Trois Romance, M/F/M]

When the rodeo rolls into town, bar owner Talia's only interest is the extra money the increase in trade will bring. What she doesn't yet know is how the sexy blond Reb and the dark, mysterious Cody will make her question everything she ever believed about men, sex and her own desires.

Not only are the cowboys lifelong buddies but they also seem to have the same taste in women--each sending her clear and persistent signals that they want her while fully aware of the interest of their friend.

Unable to resist the lure of her own private rodeo, she succumbs to the cowboys' overwhelming mutual seduction. The relationship intensifies, sparking a rivalry between the friends that forces Talia to choose between them.

As the Rodeo leaves town again, will Talia have nothing but hot memories to remember it by--or will she be giving the cowboy of her dreams a Midnight Rodeo of his own?

ADULT EXCERPT

Reb smiled, smoothing a finger over her cheek before allowing it to trail down to the nipple poking through her top.

'Whoa, guys. I don't know if I can do this,' she said, taking a step back. Cody wrapped a hand around her wrist gently, stopping her flight.

'Why not?'

'Why not?' she repeated feeling cornered. 'Well, I barely know you for a start.'

'We both want you, Talia,' Reb said, running a hand down her other arm. 'We've been watching you all night,' he breathed, pulling her closer, 'watching your lovely dark hair brush over your body and that sexy little ass swaying back and forth under our noses.'

'And we know you want us,' Cody said, sliding his hand across the small of her back, urging her closer. 'I saw the way you looked at me earlier and how you reacted when Reb touched you. Your nipples got hard instantly, just like they are now.'

Talia laughed nervously. 'Look, guys. It's not that I don't find the idea appealing—but it's just not my kind of thing, ok?'

'Why, because you're a good girl?' Reb teased, running a hand over her ass. 'Or is it because you are afraid people will find out.'

'A bit of both,' she said, her resolve starting to weaken as the men pulled her between them, pressing her forward into Cody's body as Reb slotted his behind. Her head began to spin as they continued to persuade her, taking turns to speak.

'It's ok to be a bad girl if you want to be, Talia,' Cody said, bunching her hair to one side to mutter hotly into her ear. 'Nobody will ever know.'

'Let us make you feel good,' Reb whispered, rubbing his erection against her ass as he moved closer. 'You know we can.'

'Don't be scared to take what you want,' Cody said, as she stared at him uncertainly. 'But if you want us to leave, just say so.' Both of the men froze, their heated breath wafting over her face and neck as they waited for her reply. 'Do you want us to leave, Talia?'

The blood rushed in her ears as her heart skipped a beat at the prospect of the pleasure that could lie ahead if she could just reach out and grab it. She dropped Cody's gaze, shaking her head. 'No, I don't want you to leave.'

'You won't be sorry, baby,' Reb said, allowing his hand to slide between her legs. 'Fuck, Cody, she is so hot and wet I can feel it through her jeans.' He gasped, sinking his teeth into her shoulder. Talia's legs shook as Cody grasped both of her breasts, biting down gently at her lip as he sucked it into his mouth.

'Where's the bedroom?' He groaned, forcing himself to end the kiss. Talia whispered her answer, barely able to find her voice.

Enjoy Excerpt from
Two Cowboys for Christie: Midnight Cowboys 2

Available at SirenPublishing.com

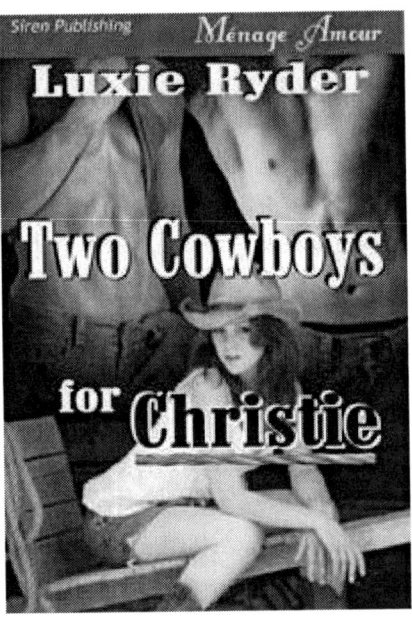

[Siren Menage Amour 47: Cowboy Menage a Trois Romance, M/F/M]

When Christie revisits her childhood home, she never dreams that her adolescent fantasies are about to become a reality.

She'd once been inseparable from the boys on the next ranch, but Garrett and Connor are all grown up and the games they want to play now aren't for kids.

When the two men make her an offer to pick up where they left off one drunken night in the barn as teenagers, Christie finds she is tempted. But who wouldn't be with two muscle bound, blue-eyed cowboys offering to make all your fantasies come true?

Christie reacts as they hope she will and a hot, steamy night ensues, leaving her with a difficult decision to make. Should she let society and her own sense of what is right and wrong keep her away from the two men she has never stopped loving and the place that is her destiny?

STORY EXCERPT

'What are you thinking about?' Garrett asked, smiling down at her softly as he refilled her glass.

'Being here again. It's so strange but it feels like I never left.'

'It doesn't feel that way for us Christie. There has always been a huge hole in our lives that only you could fill.'

'Don't say that, Garrett.'

'Why not?'

Christie put her glass down. 'Because you guys have done nothing but put pressure on me since I arrived, acting as if your whole happiness depends on how I respond to your crazy offer. You want me to stay here with you—both of you—and God help me but I've been considering it.'

'Glad to hear it,' Connor said with a smile. 'What's the problem?'

'The problem is what kind of woman would that make me?' She laughed as the absurd thoughts she'd been having spilled out of her mouth. 'You don't even know me anymore. The person you want is the naïve little kid who thought you two were gods made flesh. I've grown up, Connor, and I need a grown up relationship.'

'That's what we are offering.'

'Have you thought it through? I mean, really? I've never even had sex with either of you yet you want me to commit to having a relationship with both of you. Do you realize how insane that sounds?'

Connor blew out a frustrated breath and Garrett paced away, running a hand through his hair as he thought on her words. Finally, he turned to her. 'Look, I admit the conversation went too far last night. I was putting the cart before the horse.'

'You can say that again,' Connor said accusingly.

'All we really want is a chance to see if what we believe is true.'

'And what's that?' she asked.

'That we are meant to be together. All of us.' Garrett sat beside her on the sofa, clasping her hands in his. 'Your entire childhood, you spent every waking moment with me and Connor. You were taken away from us at a time when we'd been fighting to keep our distance because we thought it was the right thing to do. Now, we want another chance to make things turn out the way they should have all along.'

'You don't have to say yes, Christie,' Connor added, taking the seat on her other side. 'But we think you feel the same way about us.'

'What do you mean?'

'Tell Garrett you don't love him.' Connor eyes fixed on hers as he dared her to speak the words.

'You know I can't,' she said finally, dropping her gaze. She heard Garrett let out a shaky breath beside her but she couldn't bring herself to look his way. A pulse beat loudly in her ears, drowning out the tense silence in the room.

'Ok, then tell me.' Christie stared at Connor again, angry almost that he could see through her so easily. She wished she could tell him that she didn't love him just to wipe the smug look off his face but she couldn't. Tears pricked her eyes as she shook her head slowly, letting him see that she was no more able to say it to him than she had been to Garrett.

'So where does that leave us?' he asked gently. Garrett remained silent, seeming content to let Connor speak, knowing his cousin had a way with words, Christie guessed. 'We are adults and we love each other. Why aren't we together?'

'I don't know. It's just wrong I guess.'

'Who says so?' Garrett asked finally. 'Who better to make the rules for our own lives than us?'

'All we are asking for is a chance to show you how great it could be,' Connor added when Christie fell silent again. 'Let us show you how much we love you, Christie.'

She sighed, sinking back against the sofa as she closed her eyes. Christie could feel them waiting for her answer. When they put it the way they had, their suggestion didn't seem unreasonable but she simply couldn't shake the idea that it was wrong. She told them so.

'Just let it go,' Connor soothed, leaning closer as the hand that had been smoothing her hair began to trail down over her cheek. He tilted her chin, giving her plenty of time to pull away as his mouth lowered to hers.

ADULT EXCERPT

Christie gasped as their lips touched, self conscious at first to be kissing him in front of Garrett until she became aware of his hand on her shoulder. Almost as soon as she felt it, he turned her towards him and away from Connor, replacing his lips with his own.

Garrett's kiss seemed deeper and more possessive, as if he was trying to claim her. She began to respond to the probing of his tongue as it forced its way into her mouth. A long dormant ache came to life in her groin, and she tested the sensation, pushing against it as she realized how aroused she'd become.

Connor's hand caressed her thigh and she felt him move closer. His other lifted her hair, giving him access to her neck. Christie felt a hard jolt of desire slam through her as his lips found her skin and he nibbled at it gently. Garrett's free hand grasped her other leg and he wrapped a large palm around it, squeezing and smoothing as he made his way nearer and nearer to her crotch. Christie felt the first, fleeting pressure against her pussy as his knuckles grazed the fabric between her legs. Her insides contracted and she felt her muscles quiver at the warm, wet sensation his touch had caused.

'Stop,' she said weakly, ripping her mouth from Garrett's and pushing them both away. 'I can't think with the two of you doing things to me.'

The men stayed put but didn't touch her. Christie looked from one to the other. Two pairs of blue eyes stared back, watching as she straightened her clothes and got to her feet. Connor slumped forward to rest his forearms on his thighs, raising his head to look up at her. Garrett fell back, his chest rising and falling rapidly as he breathed heavily. His erection was clearly outlined in the denim of his jeans and she had to resist the urge to drop to her knees and release it.

'So, what's it gonna be, Christie?' he asked quietly, drawing her attention back to his face. 'If you keep looking at me like that, the choice isn't gonna be yours for much longer.'

'I can't have sex with both of you at once,' she protested weakly, knowing that she very much wanted to.

'That night back in the barn, we all started something we've just got to finish,' Connor said, getting to his feet to stand in front of her. 'None of us can move on until we do.'

'Besides,' Garrett added, 'it would cause too much jealousy if you chose one of us over the other. That's why we agreed, if it ever happened, it was gonna be all or nothing.'

'What makes you think I could handle that?' Christie asked

'It wouldn't have to be this way every time,' Connor said. 'Just this first time—then we'll see what happens.'

'This isn't just about sex,' Garrett said, getting to his feet to stand in front of her beside Connor, 'but I've had a hard-on for you for fifteen years and I can't wait another minute to fuck you and I know he feels the same.'

Christie got wetter. Garrett didn't know how to sweet talk a girl but if the look in his eye was anything to go by, he sure knew how to make her feel wanted. Her breath caught in her throat as she looked up at the pair of them. Every fantasy she'd ever had could be about to unfold in front of her and for the first time, she acknowledged to herself that it was exactly what she wanted. The damp throbbing in her pussy could not be ignored any longer.

She took a step back, enjoying a brief moment of power as she saw a fleeting look of disappointment cross their faces. 'Give me five minutes and then come up to my room.'

[Menage Amour 74: Erotic Western Contemporary Menage a Trois Romance, M/F/M]

Sadie wants to be just like the guys. She longs to join them in the rodeo ring, riding the broncos and bringing down steers. But her friends, Kyle and Gabe, have strong objections. Unable to understand why they refuse to help her, Sadie's frustration boils over, resulting in a wild night in the bar that forces them all to reassess their relationships with each other. Embarrassed by her behavior, Sadie is shocked to learn that rather than ruin the friendship, she has simply reignited the sexual interest they've had in her since the day she arrived in Hurley.

Learning how to ride a bull is the last thing on her mind while she has her hands full with two sexy cowboys. She's determined not to let their relationship with her return to a platonic state.

One sassy woman. Two rugged cowboys. Three for the Rodeo!

STORY EXCERPT

Gabe hissed in an amused breath as Kyle nearly spat his mouthful of beer across the room. He wiped his face as he laughed quietly. 'Do you really think this is the place for that kind of talk, Miss Perkins?'

'Well, you were talking about it already,' she said defensively, refusing to allow their amused gazes to make her feel even more stupid than she did already. 'That's what you were saying, wasn't it? You asked if he thought that woman would go home with the both of you.'

The humor left Gabe's face to be replaced with the quiet watchfulness that was always there whenever she caught him looking her way. He held her eyes for a moment longer before dropping his head as he answered. 'Why do you care?'

'I don't,' she said, picking up her beer and turning her back on them before the conversation became even more personal. Sadie wished she'd never opened her mouth. It had only been a few days since she'd turned them down on their outrageous offer, and she guessed she'd just gotten her answer as to whether it was too early to test out if they were all still friends or not. They'd given her a wide berth since that night. Both guys seemed polite enough, but the camaraderie they'd shared seemed to have gone.

Sadie gave up trying to make friends with them for the time being and moved away to the other end of the bar. Not that either of them seemed to care. Their eyes had fixed firmly on the pretty little brunette who'd just noticed the two sexy cowboys watching her. The last thing Sadie needed was to watch Kyle and Gabe seduce someone right under her nose.

Sadie took a seat, determined to focus on the band playing that night and ignore the pair until they'd at least apologized for being so mean to her. She didn't have to wait too long before she felt a strong, heavy hand on her shoulder.

'Aw, don't be sore, honey. We're sorry.' Kyle sounded sincere.

'Ok.' She sighed, making room for them as they sat on either side of her. They fell into an awkward silence that lasted about as long as it took Gabe to swallow down the rest of his beer.

'What are you doing here anyway?' he asked. Sadie scanned the cowboy's green eyes for signs of the irritation she could hear in his voice yet he wore the expression of a guy simply asking a polite question. But with Gabe, nothing was simple.

'I missed you guys,' she said, trying to make her answer less revealing with a carefree shrug. 'I hadn't seen you since the night you…you know.'

'Yeah, we know.' Gabe smiled dryly. With his light brown, sun-streaked hair and sparkling green eyes, he looked nothing like the hard, sexy man she knew him to be. Gabriel P. Miles was one hell of a rodeo rider and one horny son-of-a-bitch when you got him fired up. Leading him on for fun wouldn't be a mistake she'd make again anytime soon.

* * * *

'It wasn't entirely our fault, you know,' Kyle said, cutting through her thoughts. 'I know we pissed you off by treating you like our kid sister, but it was your decision to up the stakes.'

'And we saved you from that guy,' Gabe reminded her gently. 'So we're not all bad.'

Sadie dropped her gaze. 'I know. I owe you both an apology, too.'

The guy he'd been referring to had pinned her against the wall as she tried to pass him on her way back from the bathroom. He'd stopped short of managing to kiss her but only because Kyle and Gabe had shown up.

'Are you sure you want another beer?' Gabe asked a little later when the conversation had finally moved on to safer ground. 'You've had a few.'

As relieved as she felt to be spending time with them again, Sadie just couldn't let them get away with treating her that way. If the price of admission back into their precious circle of friendship was that she had to allow them to monitor her every move, they could forget it. Kyle had been almost as bad as Gabe, looking at her with concern every time she lifted her beer bottle to her lips. Ok, so she'd been drinking a little fast, but she felt incredibly nervous.

'I'm not a kid,' she said with as much indignation as she could muster. 'And I don't need anyone watching out for me.'

'You're not a kid, huh?' Gabe said with a smile that didn't reach his eyes. 'Could have fooled me.'

'What do you mean?'

He dropped her gaze. 'Forget it.'

'No, I won't forget it. What do you mean?'

His bottle hit the bar hard, splashing beer over his wrist. 'You really don't want to hear it, lady.'

ADULT EXCERPT

'Calm down,' Kyle warned him.

Gabe looked at her again. 'Maybe you'd better go.'

'Why?' Kyle said, saving her from asking the same question.

'Because I couldn't handle it if you changed your mind. I've spent so much time fantasizing about that night and, now you're here, all I want to do is pin you to the wall and ram my cock into you over and over again.' The words came out in an angry rush until he paused for breath, running his hands through his light brown hair as his chest heaved. 'But despite all that, if I can't be sure you are agreeing to this for the right reasons, then I think you'd better leave.'

He sank to the bed, flopping back onto it as he fought to calm himself. Sadie sat in shock, fire coursing through her as she stared at his body until Kyle's words to Gabe reached through her fog.

'Buddy, I feel the same way but you gotta take it easy.' His eyes found hers. 'It's all up to Sadie now.' He kept his composure better than his friend but she didn't doubt his feelings ran as deeply. His body sank back against the counter and his groin got hard under her gaze, as if she'd really touched him. The challenge in his eyes darkened them to an inky black, and she heard a hiss as he sucked in a breath and bit down into his bottom lip while he waited for her to make a move.

Sadie did move, but not in his direction. She shrugged off the jogging suit she wore and got down to her nightshirt before she dared another look at either of them. Kyle's eyes began to glitter possessively, but he wasn't her priority at that moment.

Gabe had her full attention. He seemed to be in torment and she wanted, or rather needed, to make it better. Kyle would take care of himself.

Gabe's body lurched upwards as he felt the first touch of her nails scraping up the denim of his thighs. His shocked expression disappeared as Sadie massaged the powerful muscles beneath her palms, shushing him when he began to speak so she could concentrate on inching nearer and nearer to his penis swelling at the crotch of his jeans.

Sliding over his body to put her full weight on him, Sadie cupped his face in her hands and looked deeply into his eyes before kissing him, so that he would know this was what she wanted. His reaction was all she could hope for. His hands came up to crush her head closer as his hot tongue forced its way between her lips.

Sadie dragged her mouth from his to sit back across his thighs and she tore the shirt from his jeans, ripping open the buttons and dragging it from his shoulders. Job done, her hands dropped to the buckle at his waist and she worked quickly to free his cock. Gabe hissed and lurched forward again as she pulled him free of his clothing. His penis was hard and thick and she felt him jerk as she ran her hand up the length of it, flicking her thumb over the top.

'Baby, slow down,' he gasped, smiling to take the edge off his words.

She laughed, feeling no embarrassment. Her sudden and drastic change of heart had surprised her almost as much as it did Gabe. 'Sorry. I kind of got carried away.'

'Don't you dare apologize,' she heard Kyle say behind her. Sadie turned to find him naked and standing at her side. In her rush to get at Gabe, she hadn't heard him move.

'Take your hat off, idiot.' Kyle didn't take offense at Gabe's words, turning to throw his hat across the room with a silly grin. Gabe took the opportunity to shrug his jeans down his legs and off his feet before pulling her back across his lap.

Kyle leaned forward to grab her nightshirt at the hem and rip it clean up over her head. She felt a moment's shyness as two sets of eyes raced over her skin but forgot it as soon as Kyle pushed her forward over Gabe's body.

Siren Publishing, Inc.
www.SirenPublishing.com

LaVergne, TN USA
20 August 2009
155395LV00004B/69/P